A Risky Business

"Just imagine, Ghost," Val sighed as he gently jog-trotted out of the barn. "By this time next month, I'll have a stepmother and a stepsister, and if Dr. Weintraub can perform the surgery very soon, maybe you'll be able to see clearly again."

If. Maybe, echoed a persistent little voice inside her head. *Remember what your father said. The operation is very risky. If it fails, The Ghost could be totally blind. Totally blind. Totally blind. Maybe you ought to reconsider. . . .*

**Look for these books
in the Animal Inn series
from Apple Paperbacks:**

ANIMAL INN

GIFT HORSE

Virginia Vail

AN
APPLE
PAPERBACK

SCHOLASTIC INC.
New York Toronto London Auckland Sydney

ISBN 0-590-42803-9

12 11 10 9 8 7 6 5 4 3 2 1   1 2 3 4 5 6/9

Printed in the U.S.A.   40

First Scholastic printing, March 1991

For Christina, Matthew, Ashley, Jonathan, Teri, Heidi, Noelle, Josh, and all the other fans of **ANIMAL INN** who have written such wonderful letters to me. Also, special thanks to Janice Liebowitz and John and Isabella Falcocchio for all their help.

Chapter 1

Peep, peep, peep, peep, peep!

The shrill cheeping of dozens of day-old chicks rang in Valentine Taylor's ears as she gently snuggled one of the tiny balls of fluff against her cheek. Val had just finished helping her veterinarian father vaccinate Roy Miller's newly hatched Leghorns. Now, while Doc treated a hen that had a mild respiratory infection, Val was enjoying watching the babies scratch around in their warm, brightly lighted enclosure. She had seen hundreds of baby chicks, but it never failed to amaze and delight her that they looked exactly like Easter cards come to life — except that Easter cards didn't make so much noise!

Very carefully, Val returned the chick she'd been holding to its relatives and friends. Only a moment later, she couldn't tell which one it was. It had become part of the little sea of yellow fluff-balls beneath the low-hanging lights. Val hoped it was a female so all it would be expected to do when it grew up would be to lay eggs. If it was a male, sooner or later it would end up as somebody's dinner. Val wanted to be a vet like her father, and she hated knowing that some of the animals she helped him care for would be eaten. That's why she couldn't bring herself to eat any kind of meat.

Bending down, she whispered to the chicks, "Good luck!"

"Want to take a couple of these little guys home with you, Vallie?" asked old Mr. Miller's son, Roy Junior. Val hadn't heard him come up behind her because the chicks were cheeping so loudly.

"Thanks, Junior, but we already have some chickens," Val said, smiling at him. She felt kind of funny calling a grown man "Junior," but everybody in Essex, Pennsylvania, called him that, so Val did, too.

"Well, if you change your mind, just say the word," Junior said. "Pop told me to ask you, so I said I would."

"Thank him for me, too. How is he?" Val asked. "Is he feeling better?" Old Mr. Miller had been sick for a long time. He hardly ever left the house, and Junior took care of running the farm for him.

Junior shrugged. "About the same, Vallie. He has good days and bad days, but most of the time he's kind of in between, if you know what I mean. He gets awful cranky sometimes because he can't ride that mare of his. I think he likes that fool horse more than he does people!"

Val knew that Mr. Miller's chestnut mare,

Dancer, was his pride and joy. It made her sad to think that the old man couldn't ride anymore, and she was sure Junior must feel sad, too.

Before she could think of something to say to make him feel better, he said, "Why don't you take a run up to the pasture and say hello to Dancer? It'd make Pop happy to know she had a visitor, 'specially if it's you. Pop says you're the only kid in Essex who really knows animals. 'Tell Vallie she can ride Dancer any time she wants to,' he told me. If you have the time, I'll show you where her saddle and bridle are."

"Gee, Junior, I'd love to," Val said. "But as soon as Dad's through with his patient, we'll have to get back to Animal Inn. The clinic opens in half an hour, and we always have a lot of animals to take care of on Saturday mornings. I have time to visit Dancer, though. Maybe some other time. . . ."

Junior nodded and headed for the part of Mr. Miller's poultry house where the sick hen had been isolated from the rest of the flock. "She'll be real glad to see you," he called over his shoulder. "I don't ride, myself — don't like horses much, to tell the truth. Guess maybe she's kind of lonely."

Val stripped off the sterilized rubber boots she was wearing to prevent infection being passed from one flock to another. She placed them neatly by the poultry house door, then trudged in her sneakers through the barnyard to the pasture not far from the Millers' farmhouse.

It was a beautiful morning in mid-April, and the grass was thick and lush. Barn swallows swooped high overhead against a cloudless blue sky. The clear, fresh air was filled with bird song, and the tall trees that grew along the pasture fence were covered with tender green leaves.

Val's spirits lifted as she approached the white-washed fence around Dancer's pasture. The six-year-old mare raised her head when she saw Val coming. Her coat was a rich reddish-brown, almost the same color as Val's hair. But instead of being sleek and shiny, it was thick and furry. Obviously, nobody had groomed her in a long time.

"Hi, Dancer," Val called. "Remember me? I haven't seen you in a while, but my dad treated you for colic a few months ago and I helped him."

The mare pricked up her ears and snorted as she ambled toward the fence. Val thought that even with her scruffy winter coat, Dancer was beautiful. *How could Junior not like horses?* she wondered. Val loved all animals but she loved horses most. Now she ducked between the fence rails and went over to pat the mare.

Running her fingers throught Dancer's tangled mane, Val said, "If you were *my* horse, you wouldn't be such a mess. You should see The Ghost — he's all sleek and shiny because I brush and curry him almost every day." The Gray Ghost was Val's fifteen-year-old dapple-gray gelding. He had been a champion jumper before he developed cataracts in both eyes. Val had used all her savings to buy him when his owner, Trevor Merrill, had wanted to have him destroyed.

Now Val began removing burrs and bits of dry grass from Dancer's mane and forelock. "I'll tell you a secret," she said to the mare. "The Essex Horsemen's Association is having a show over the Fourth of July weekend, and I'm going to enter The Ghost in the Open Jumper competition!"

Dancer tossed her head and whuffled as though she were surprised to hear Val's news.

"I know," Val said. "Everybody thinks he can't see well enough to jump anymore, and he can't — not yet. But ever since I bought The Ghost from Mr. Merrill and his awful daughter, Cassandra, I've been saving up to pay for an operation to remove his cataracts. Even though Dad's a wonderful vet, he doesn't have the special equipment to perform the surgery. But he knows a vet in Philadelphia who specializes in equine ophthalmology — that means treating eye problems in horses," she said. (Though Val was convinced that animals understood what people said to them, she figured that technical terms needed to be explained.)

"I haven't told Dad yet how much money I've saved, but I'm going to do it today," she went on. "And I'm going to ask him to call Dr. Weintraub and make an appointment for us to bring The Ghost to Philadelphia for the operation. By July, he'll be completely recovered, and Mr. Merrill and Cassandra will realize that they made a big mistake when they wanted Dad to put him to sleep!"

Dancer butted Val playfully with her head, and Val laughed. "Okay, okay! I won't pull any more burrs out of your mane. But I bet your tail's in even worse shape. Will you let me see what I can do? You won't kick me or anything, will you?"

But before she could tackle the mare's tail, Val heard the honking of the Animal Inn van. Apparently her father had finished treating Mr. Miller's ailing hen and was ready to go back to the clinic.

Val patted Dancer's neck, raising a cloud of dust. "Sorry, Dancer," she said. "Gotta go now. See you soon, okay?"

Dancer followed Val to the fence and watched her slip through the rails again and run off across the field to where Doc Taylor's dark blue van was parked by the barnyard. Just before Val climbed into the passenger seat, she turned and waved to the chestnut mare. She thought Dancer looked sorry to see her go.

"What did Dancer have to say?" Doc Taylor teased as he backed the van down the dirt road that led to Essex Drive. "Did you two have a nice conversation?"

"As a matter of fact, we did," Val said, grinning at her father. "It was kind of one-sided, but that was okay. I think Dancer was happy to have somebody pay some attention to her for once. How's Mr. Miller's hen?"

"She's going to be fine. None of the other chickens will be infected. Roy Miller runs a clean farm — or rather, Junior does." Doc turned the van onto Essex Drive, heading for Animal Inn. "We ought to be just in time for our first appointment. And if we're a few minutes late, Toby can handle it."

Toby Curran was Doc's other young assistant. At fourteen, he was only a year older than Val, and was one of her best friends.

"Dad, listen!" Val said eagerly. "Remember when I bought The Ghost and you told me you knew somebody who might be able to save his sight?"

Doc nodded. "Aaron Weintraub. Yes, I remember. Why?"

"Well, it's time for him to do it!" Hazel eyes shining, Val turned to her father. "I've saved up a thousand dollars, and I want The Ghost to have that operation!"

Doc glanced at her in surprise. "A thousand dollars? Honey, I'm really impressed! You're probably the only teenager in town with so much money of her own."

Val shook her head. "No way. Cassandra Merrill probably has *millions*, and to hear Lila Bascombe talk, you'd think she did, too!" Lila was in Val's class at Hamilton Junior High, but the two girls didn't like each other very much. It drove Val crazy to hear Lila brag about how rich her family was. And it drove her even crazier when Lila made fun of Val's "old blind horse."

"That's not the same thing," Doc said. "Whatever money Cassandra and Lila have actually belongs to their parents. But you've worked very hard to *earn* your money, and I'm proud of you."

His praise made Val feel good all over. She smiled at him. "Thanks, Dad. So will you do it? Get in touch with Dr. Weintraub, I mean? If he can operate on The Ghost real soon, I'm going to enter him in the Horsemen's Association's show!"

"Well now, Vallie, I don't know about that," her father said very solemnly. "I think Dr. Weintraub would look pretty silly trotting around the show ring in a saddle and bridle!"

"Oh, Dad!" Val giggled. "You know what I mean. I want to enter *The Ghost* in the horse show, not the doctor! I know he'll never be really happy if he never jumps again, and I want to give him the chance to prove that he's still a champion. I'm sure the reason The Ghost has been off his feed lately is because he misses being able to jump. You said yourself when you examined him the other day that there's nothing physically wrong with him."

"That's true," Doc said. "But I'm not convinced that he's pining for another blue ribbon to add to his collection. And remember, Vallie, there's no guarantee that the surgery will be successful. An operation of this kind on a horse as old as The Ghost is very risky."

"It couldn't kill him, could it?" Val asked.

"No. But it's entirely possible that the result will

be total blindness. Granted, The Ghost's vision is slowly getting worse, but there's every indication that without the operation he'll be able to see fairly well for a number of years yet. He may eventually go blind, but in the meantime — "

"In the meantime, he can't jump," Val interrupted. "Remember when we saw him in the Harrisburg Horse Show? I was only around eight years old but I'll never, *ever* forget how wonderful he was. He sailed over those fences as if he had wings! I could tell how much he loved it from the way he pricked up his ears and swished his tail. If there's any chance at all that he could be that happy again, he deserves it. And boy, would I love to see the look on Cassandra Merrill's face when she finds out that the horse she sold me for two hundred dollars is still a champion!"

"Aren't you forgetting something, honey?" her father asked.

Val frowned. "What?"

"A champion jumper needs a champion rider, and you've never learned how to jump," he pointed out gently.

"I'll learn," Val said. "I'll take lessons! After all, The Ghost's so good that all I'll really have to learn is how to stay on when he goes over the jumps. Oh, Dad, will you *please* call Dr. Weintraub? Please?"

Doc reached over and patted her hand. "All right, Vallie. I'll try to reach him today, and we'll see what he has to say."

Val beamed. "Terrific! I can't wait to tell Lila that I'm entering The Ghost in the horse show. She may have a prize-winning poodle, but that's nothing compared to a prize-winning horse!"

"Don't get your hopes up too high," Doc warned, pulling the van into the parking lot in front of Animal Inn. "And don't count your chickens before they're hatched — or your ribbons before they're won. We don't even know yet if Dr. Weintraub will be available to perform the surgery at all. And if he *is* available, remember what I said. The operation may leave The Ghost worse off than he is now."

"But at least he'll have a chance," Val said dreamily. "A chance to be a champion again, even if it's only in a local show."

"Wake up, honey," Doc said with a smile as they got out of the van. "Judging from the number of cars here, we have a busy morning ahead of us. Funny — according to my appointment book, Miss Kleindinst was bringing Pussum in at nine to be treated for ear mites, and my next patient isn't due until nine-thirty."

Val checked her watch. "It's only nine-fifteen. Maybe Miss Vickers brought Sprinkles in early. And the other two cars might belong to people who have appointments with Donna Hartman to groom their pets."

"If that's the case, they're *really* early," Doc said, striding up the path to the one-story brick building that housed the Small Animal Clinic. "The grooming salon doesn't open until ten. Come to think of it," he added, "I believe that red station wagon belongs to Mayor Anderson, and he doesn't have any pets. I wonder what he's doing here."

"Gee, I hope nothing's wrong," Val said.

Doc shrugged. "There's only one way to find out." He opened the door to the waiting room, and he and Val stepped inside.

Chapter
2

"Well, here's the future bridegroom now!" Mayor Anderson said heartily, coming over to shake Doc's hand. "And about time, too. For Catherine's sake, I hope you're not going to be late for your wedding!"

Glancing at Doc, Val saw that his face was turning red above his short, graying beard. Her widowed father still wasn't used to all the attention he'd been getting ever since he and Catherine Sparks had announced their engagement at Miss Maggie Rafferty's Christmas party. Neither was Val, though she had always known how popular Doc was. Catherine had moved to Essex less than a year ago, but she had made many friends as well, and so had her little daughter, Sparky. In fact, Sparky was one of eight-year-old Teddy Taylor's very best friends.

Because everybody in town liked Doc and Catherine so much, they were all delighted to learn that the couple were to be married in mid-May. And they all seemed determined to turn the wedding into a major celebration, though both Catherine and Doc were equally determined to keep it a small, family affair.

"Oh, I'll be on time for that, all right," Doc told the mayor with a grin. "Vallie and I are running a little late today because we had to stop by Roy Miller's farm. Sorry about that, Miss Kleindinst," he said to the plump, middle-aged woman who was sitting on one of the benches. She was holding her big striped cat on her lap. Pussum didn't look very happy, but Miss Kleindinst did.

"That's perfectly all right, Doc," she said, smiling. "Pussum and I don't mind a bit, do we, Pussum?" Pussum looked as if he minded a lot, Val thought. "We know how busy you are. And you must be even busier with the wedding only four weeks away."

"I think it's just wonderful that you and Mrs. Sparks are getting married, Dr. Taylor," added Miss Vickers, and her springer spaniel yelped as if to say that he thought it was wonderful, too. Miss Vickers was Teddy's and Sparky's third-grade teacher. "Mrs. Sparks is such a lovely woman. I'm sure you'll be very happy together. My class has already started a special arts-and-crafts project for a wedding present, but it's supposed to be a big surprise so I can't tell you what it is."

Val had gone over to the reception desk where Toby was sitting, and now he looked up at her and grinned. "I bet it'll be a surprise, all right," he whispered. "She'll probably have to tell your dad and Catherine what it is *after* the kids give it to them!" Val couldn't help giggling.

"Speaking of the wedding," said a short, sandy-haired man who had been fidgeting impatiently while the others spoke, "I just stopped by to drop off some information about my catering service." He thrust a folder bulging with papers under Doc's nose. "Fred's Fabulous Food. I'm Fred, Fred Snyder. My outfit catered the Humane Society banquet back in February. Maybe you remember one of the dishes—pork cutlets with apricot-sauerkraut sauce?"

"I remember it very well, Mr. Snyder," Doc said dryly. "I'd never tasted anything like it in my life. But — "

"Our specialty is festive occasions like your upcoming nuptials," Mr. Snyder went on before Doc could continue. "Now, since you and your intended are getting married before the June rush, I can offer you an excellent rate for around two hundred guests, wedding cake included, of course — "

This time Doc cut him off. "Wait a minute!" he said, holding up a hand. "We're planning on a much smaller reception than that."

"Well then, I can give you a good deal on between a hundred and a hundred and fifty," Mr. Snyder said. "Large or small, makes no difference to me."

"*Small*," Doc said. "Very, *very* small. My fiancée and I have decided on a simple ceremony with only our children and a few close friends in attendance. And my housekeeper will provide the refreshments, so I'm afraid you're wasting your time."

He tried to give the folder back to Mr. Snyder, but Mayor Anderson stepped forward. "Now, hold on there, Ted. You're not serious, are you?" he said, staring at Doc.

"I certainly am. Catherine and I agree that, since we've both been married before, we want to do this with a minimum of fuss and bother," Doc told him.

The mayor put an arm around his shoulders. "Ted, you can't *do* this to your friends and neighbors," he said earnestly. "You can't shut them out of this important milestone in your lives! You're one of our town's most respected citizens, and we're all very fond of Catherine, too. It's your civic *duty* to allow us all to participate."

"Oh, brother," Val murmured to Toby. "It sounds like he's making one of his campaign speeches!"

"That's why I came here this morning," Mayor Anderson went on. "To tell you that I'm putting the town hall at your disposal for the wedding and the reception."

"The *town hall?*" Doc echoed. "Bill, I . . ."

"No need to thank me," the mayor said, slapping him on the back. "Talk it over with Catherine and let me know within the next few days. I'll be going now — it's a great day for golf!"

"I'm on my way, too," said Mr. Snyder. "After

you've discussed your plans with the little woman, give me a call. I can give you a *fantastic* rate for three hundred guests or more!"

As the big, hefty mayor and the small, thin caterer went out the door, Miss Kleindinst heaved a huge sigh. "Three hundred guests! Imagine that! It's going to be the biggest wedding Essex has ever seen, isn't it, Pussum?"

Pussum growled and scratched at his ears.

"It's just so *romantic*," Miss Vickers burbled. "I always dreamed of having a big wedding — I think every woman does. And the town hall will look just lovely filled with hundreds and hundreds of flowers!"

"Miss Kleindinst, Miss Vickers, please try to understand," Doc said, turning from one woman to the other. "Catherine and I are *not* going to be married in the town hall!"

"Of course you're not!" said Miss Maggie Rafferty, striding into the waiting room. As usual, she was wearing a work shirt and men's trousers tucked into sturdy boots, and her long, gray-streaked brown hair was in an untidy knot on top of her head. Although Miss Maggie was somewhere in her eighties, she had the energy and spunk of a woman half her age.

Val was happy to see her. Miss Maggie was one of her favorite people. "Hi, Miss Maggie," she cried.

"Morning, Valentine. Morning, Toby." Miss Maggie nodded at Miss Kleindinst and Miss Vickers, then marched right over to Doc. "Town hall indeed!"

she blustered. "What a ridiculous notion! Who in their right mind would want to be married in that stuffy old place with all those bad portraits of stodgy old mayors looking on? Willie Anderson ought to have his head examined and I told him so only yesterday!"

"*Willie?*" Toby snorted with laughter.

Miss Maggie shot him an amused glance from her bright blue eyes. "That's what he was called when he was in my third-grade class, and that's how I think of him to this day." She turned back to Doc. "Now about this wedding, young Theodore. I couldn't agree with you more. The town hall is definitely *out*."

"It certainly is," Doc said. "I'm glad you understand."

"Of course I do. And I have the perfect alternative." She smiled broadly. "You and Catherine will be married on my estate! The weather is sure to be fine on May fifteenth, and I have acres of lawn just going to waste. There's plenty of room for at least four hundred guests. And don't worry about the expense. I'll take care of the whole thing myself. What's the use of being the richest woman in Essex if I can't do a favor for my friends?"

Val and Toby gaped at each other and each mouthed the words, "Four hundred guests?"

"*Four hundred guests?*" Doc said. "Miss Maggie — *dear* Miss Maggie, I appreciate your generous offer, believe me I do. But what Catherine and I want is a *very small* wedding and reception. The only guests we plan to invite are you, Toby, Donna Hartman and her husband Jim, Pat Dempwolf, Mike Strickler, and Mrs. Racer and her son, Henry." Pat was his receptionist during the week. Mike took care of the animals in the infirmary, the Large Animal Clinic, and the boarding kennel after office hours and on Sundays and Mondays when Animal Inn was closed. And Mrs. Racer was the Taylors' housekeeper.

"Nonsense!" Miss Maggie snapped. "What kind of a way is that to start your new life together? I happen to know that Catherine's first wedding wasn't much to write home about — she told me at my Christmas party that she was disappointed. And she was also disappointed in the marriage, which doesn't surprise me one bit. The only good thing that came out of it is Sparky, and since the divorce, that little girl needs a father. She needs *you*, Theodore, and she needs a big celebration, too. So I don't want to hear any more about it."

"Thank you, Miss Maggie," Doc mumbled. "I'll talk to Catherine about it and we'll let you know very soon."

"Good!" Miss Maggie tucked a stray strand of hair behind her ear and headed for the door, her boots clumping on the linoleum floor.

Val watched through a window as she climbed into the donkey cart behind Pedro, the little burro she had rescued from a farmer who had treated him badly. Miss Maggie had never learned to drive a car and avoided riding in them as well. Though she could have well afforded to keep a limousine and driver, she refused to add more pollution to the atmosphere.

"That old lady is something else," Toby said, peering through the window over Val's shoulder.

"She sure is," Val agreed.

Then she heard her father say, "Miss Kleindinst, I apologize again for keeping you and Pussum waiting. Vallie, please bring Pussum into the first treatment room. Miss Vickers, this shouldn't take very long. I'll be with you in a few minutes."

"Four hundred guests!" Miss Kleindinst breathed as Val picked up her cat. "That's the biggest wedding I've ever heard of."

"Me, too," Val sighed. "Now, Pussum, you cut that out! Stop digging your claws into my shoulder. I know your ears itch, but Dad will fix you up in no time flat."

As she carried Miss Kleindinst's cat into the first treatment room, Val wondered how her father and Catherine were going to handle all these offers of help in planning their wedding. They certainly wouldn't want to hurt anyone's feelings, most especially not Miss Maggie's. But on the other hand, they didn't want to be the main attraction in a three-ring circus, either. Val just hoped that Doc wouldn't get so involved in wedding worries that he forgot to call Dr. Weintraub about The Ghost!

* * *

Doc didn't forget. But he was unable to reach Dr. Weintraub at his clinic or at home, much to Val's disappointment. The doctor had gone away for the weekend and wouldn't be back until Tuesday morning. Doc promised Val he would call again then, so she had to be satisfied with that.

During her lunch break, Val looked through the pages of the Essex phone book for a riding instructor. There was only one listed, a woman named Paula Morgan. When Val called, she learned that Ms. Morgan's pupils took their lessons on her horses, not their own. She was dismayed to find out how expensive the lessons were — twenty-five dollars an hour for basic horsemanship, and thirty-five for jumping lessons. But Val made an appointment for a week from Sunday anyway.

After she hung up, she did some quick figuring on one of Doc's scratch pads. Until now, she had deposited half the salary she earned at Animal Inn into her savings account at the Farmers and Mechanics Bank and Trust. But she wouldn't have to do that anymore. That meant she'd have enough money for twelve lessons before the horse show.

"Twelve lessons!" Val said aloud, smiling. "That's great! By the Fourth of July, I bet I'll be as good a rider as Cassandra Merrill. Maybe better!"

Then another thought struck her and her smile faded. "But if I spend all my money on riding lessons, I won't be able to buy a wedding present for Dad and Catherine." Looking at her figures again, Val decided to take only ten lessons. Then she would have about a hundred dollars left over.

"Maybe I won't be *quite* as good as Cassandra with only ten lessons," she murmured. "But I can get a really super gift! Now all I have to do is decide what it's going to be."

Toby stuck his head in the doorway of Doc's office. "Since when did you start talking to yourself?" he teased. He came over to the desk and looked down at the pad Val had been scribbling on. "Math homework?"

Val shook her head. "Nope. Just trying to figure out how much money I can spend on a wedding present." She wasn't ready to tell Toby about The Ghost's operation, or that she planned to ride him in the horse show. She didn't want to tell anybody, not even her best friend, Jill Dearborne, until Doc had made the appointment with Dr. Weintraub. But then she'd tell everybody in town!

"What are you going to get?" Toby asked.

"I don't know yet," Val admitted. "It's a real problem. Between them, they have just about everything. Catherine's even getting rid of a lot of her stuff because she and Sparky will be moving in with us after the wedding. We sure don't need two toasters and two mixers and two microwaves and two — "

"I get the point," Toby said. "You're right — it's a problem. I've been trying to think of what to give them, too." Suddenly he brightened. "Hey, what about this? D'you think they'd like a cow?"

"A *cow?*" Val repeated.

"Sure! My heifer, Daisy, won first prize in the 4-H competition at the county fair last fall. She's a real good milker, too. And she could live in the Large Animal Clinic with The Ghost when she's not out to pasture."

"Gee, Toby, that's a real neat idea," Val said. "But I don't think Catherine knows much about cows. I don't even know if she *likes* cows very much."

Toby's rather large ears began to turn pink, a sure sign that he was upset. "Why wouldn't she? What's she got against cows, anyway?"

"Nothing at all," Val said quickly. "I'm sure she'd love Daisy once she got to know her. It's just that — well, I think a wedding present should be something both people can share and enjoy. And somehow I can't see Catherine and Dad sharing a cow."

Toby's shoulders slumped. "I guess you've got a point. I'll try to come up with some other ideas."

Val grinned at him. "So far, you're way ahead of me. I haven't even come up with *one!* But we still have four whole weeks. That gives us plenty of time to think of something extra-special."

"Yeah," said Toby. "And I bet everybody else in Essex is doing the same thing. If they get married at Miss Maggie's like she said, there're gonna be an awful lot of wedding presents! Maybe Catherine should keep on renting her house on Walnut Street just to store all the junk they're gonna get."

Val's eyes widened. "Wow! I hadn't thought about that part of it! Let's see . . ." She began scribbling on the pad again. "If four hundred people come to the wedding and the reception, probably half of them will be couples or families. And if each couple or family brings a gift, that means at least two hundred presents!"

"That's a lot of stuff," Toby said. "Maybe instead of giving them something, I oughta offer to take something away."

"I don't think Dad and Catherine are going to be very happy about this," Val said with a sigh.

Chapter
3

"I have a fantastic idea," Doc said that evening. "Catherine, let's elope!"

The Taylors, Catherine, and Sparky were sitting at the picnic table in the Sparkses' backyard, eating Chinese take-out that Doc and Val had picked up on their way back from Animal Inn.

Stabbing at a piece of sweet-and-sour pork with her chopsticks, Catherine said, "You know something? That *is* a fantastic idea! I wonder why we didn't think of it before."

"*Elope?*" said Val's eleven-year-old sister, Erin. "You mean run off and get married all by yourselves? You're kidding, aren't you? Mrs. Racer just started making the bridesmaids' dresses for Vallie, Sparky, and me! They're going to be just beautiful, too. You picked out the fabric and the pattern yourself, Catherine!"

"I know," Catherine sighed. "But that was when I still thought that your father and I could get away with a nice, quiet family wedding. Now it looks as if that's impossible." She ran her fingers through her short, brown hair. "Vallie, give me one of those plastic forks. I can't cope with chopsticks tonight."

Val rummaged through the paper bags and found a fork, which she handed to her future stepmother. She knew that Catherine had had a rough day. With the help of Teddy, Sparky, and Erin, Catherine had been sorting and packing her belongings, separating the things she would no longer need from those she couldn't do without. Because she had a full-time job as a paralegal in a lawyer's office, she had only evenings and weekends to prepare for her new life.

"Mom, if you and Doc elope, we'll never have a chance to wear those pretty dresses," Sparky mumbled around a mouthful of fried rice.

"Gimme a break!" Teddy groaned. "I can't believe how dopey you're acting, Sparky! Eric and Billy and me almost forgot you're a girl 'cause you didn't fool around with dolls and clothes and stuff. But now all you do is hang out with Erin, talking about what you're gonna wear to the wedding. Go ahead and elope, Dad. Then maybe Sparky'll start acting like Sparky again!"

Doc smiled. "Sorry, Teddy. I'm afraid you'll have to put up with wedding fever for a while longer, since it seems to have infected everybody we know. Much as Catherine and I would like to sneak off and get married, our friends just wouldn't understand."

"Oh, good!" Erin exclaimed happily. "I'm so

glad you were only teasing, because I think a big, fancy wedding sounds wonderful! And Miss Maggie's estate is so beautiful in the spring. You could be married in her rose garden and Vallie, Sparky, and I could carry little baskets filled with rose petals and sprinkle them as we walk down the garden path!"

"I don't think Miss Maggie's roses will be blooming by May fifteenth," Val pointed out. "And to tell you the truth, Erin, I'd feel pretty silly throwing flower petals around."

"You'd *look* pretty silly, too," Teddy grumbled. "And if anybody thinks *I'm* gonna do a dumb thing like that, they can just forget it, that's all!"

But Erin was so caught up in her fantasy that she paid no attention to either of them. "It'll be just like Aurora's wedding in *Sleeping Beauty*," she said dreamily. "That's one of my favorite ballets. When I'm a ballerina like Mommy was, I'll dance Princess Aurora the way she did." She turned to Catherine. "Come to think of it, if you got married in the town hall instead of at Miss Maggie's, I could wear my toe shoes! I could come down the aisle *en pointe*, scattering rose petals over all the guests! I couldn't do that on Miss Maggie's lawn. . . ."

"Honey, your dumplings are getting cold," Doc told her. "Finish your supper, okay? And do me a favor — please don't get your heart set on a monster wedding with hundreds of guests. Neither Catherine nor I can handle it."

"We certainly can't," Catherine said wearily.

"But we have to figure out what we're going to do very soon. The invitations ought to go out within the next two weeks, but I can't send them if I don't know who we're inviting."

"Hey, Mom, you never showed me the invitations," Sparky said. "Can we all see them now?"

"No, Philomena, because I haven't even ordered them yet!" her mother confessed. "And I can't order them until I know how many we'll need. And I won't know how many we'll need until we decide how many people we're inviting." She sighed. "Oh, dear, I seem to be talking in circles!"

Doc put his arm around her. "You're right — you *are* talking in circles. Let's change the subject, all right? We're both frazzled and we're not thinking straight. We'll tackle the problem tomorrow of how to get married without offending most of our friends and neighbors. Right now, I'm ready for a fortune cookie."

"Me, too!" Teddy cried. "Only I don't know why they call them *fortune* cookies. They don't have any money in them, just little pieces of paper that tell you what's supposed to happen to you."

"There's more than one kind of fortune, Teddy," Val told him, digging into one of the paper bags. "There's money, and then there's your fate." She started handing out the cookies.

Sparky broke hers open right away. "Mine says, 'A tall, handsome stranger will become very important in your life'!" Her brown eyes grew as big as saucers. "Wow! That's gotta be you, Doc. You're not a stranger anymore, but you were when Mom and I first met you. And you're tall and handsome, too!"

"Thank you for the compliment," Doc said, laughing.

Catherine laughed, too. "I can't wait to read mine," she said. She drew the slip of paper out of her cookie and read aloud, " 'The decision you are about to make will affect your future in many ways.' Well, that's certainly true! Vallie, what does yours say?"

Cracking open her fortune cookie, Val read the message. " 'You will achieve your heart's desire.' "

Erin frowned. "That's awfully general. It could mean anything."

Val just smiled. She was perfectly satisfied with her fortune. Her heart's desire was for The Ghost to regain his sight so he could compete in the July horse show, but nobody knew about that except Doc. "Read yours, Dad," she suggested.

"Okay, here goes." Doc made a big production of removing his fortune and waving it around before he read the words, " 'Help! I'm being held prisoner in a Chinese bakery!' "

Everybody broke up.

"I still wish there were *real* fortunes in these cookies," Teddy said, tugging on the visor of the Phillies baseball cap he always wore. "The money kind. Then we'd all be really rich!"

"Even if we were, we'd still have a major problem to solve," Catherine said. "Fortune cookies can't tell your father and me how to keep everybody in Essex happy if we don't invite them all to our wedding. That's something we have to work out on our own."

"So what are they going to do?" Jill Dearborne asked Val the following afternoon. The two girls had spent the past couple of hours carrying some of Val's belongings up to her new room. Sparky would be moving into her old room after Doc and Catherine were married, and Val was thrilled to have the whole third floor to herself. Now Val and Jill were taking a break, sitting in the tree house Doc had built in the apple tree in the Taylors' backyard. The scent of pinkish-white blossoms filled their nostrils, and Cleveland, Val's big orange cat, was curled up in her lap.

"About the wedding, I mean," Jill went on.

"Beats me," Val said with a shrug. "Mayor Anderson wants Dad and Catherine to be married in the town hall, and Miss Maggie wants them to have the wedding on her estate. And they're not the only ones with suggestions. Just about everybody who comes to Animal Inn has an idea about it, and they all expect to be invited." She tickled Cleveland under his chin. "But Catherine and Dad don't want a whole lot of fuss, and neither do Teddy and I. Erin's the one who thinks a huge wedding would be neat, and I think Sparky agrees with her."

Jill flopped down on the floor of the tree house, gazing up at the blossoms overhead. "It's funny how things work out, isn't it?" she said. "Erin didn't want your father ever to get married again, but now she's all excited about it. And Sparky used to be such a tomboy! Somehow I just can't picture her wearing one of those ruffly dresses Mrs. Racer is making."

"Yeah, I know. A lot of things have changed, all right," Val said. "At first, Teddy and I didn't want Dad to marry Catherine, either. After Mom died in that awful car accident three years ago, none of us could imagine anybody taking her place. But Catherine understands how we feel, and she doesn't try to act like she's our real mother. She's more like a grown-up friend. We all like her a lot."

Jill smiled. "I'm glad, because I do, too. So do my mom and dad."

"Sparky hasn't really changed, though," Val told her. "She's still a tomboy, but she's so happy about having Dad for a stepfather that she doesn't mind getting into a dress for just one day."

Jill picked up a fallen apple blossom and tucked it into her short blonde curls. "Most of the time I like being an only child, but sometimes I think it would be nice to have a big family like yours."

Grinning, Val said, "Well, whenever you start feeling lonely, you're welcome to come over and join the crowd."

"Haven't you noticed? I already do!" Jill sat up and reached out to pat Cleveland, who had fallen asleep in Val's lap. "Cleveland's been an only cat all his life. I wonder how he'll react when Sparky's cat, Charlie, moves in."

Val shrugged. "Your guess is as good as mine. I don't think he'll be very happy about it, and neither will the dogs. But they'll just have to get used to it. Right now, that's the least of our problems. First Dad and Catherine have to decide whether to have the kind of wedding they want, or the kind everyone else thinks they should have."

"That's a real problem," Jill agreed. "They certainly don't want to hurt anybody's feelings, particularly not Miss Maggie's. Too bad Essex is such a small town where everybody knows everybody else's business." She giggled. "My dad says that if you sneeze in Essex, a dozen people all over town say 'God bless you!' "

Val laughed, too. "That sounds like something *my* dad would say!" She draped her cat over her shoulder and stood up.

"*Mrraaow?*" Cleveland said, opening one sleepy yellow eye.

"Sorry, Cleveland, but we can't stay here all afternoon," Val told him. "Jill and I have work to do. Come on, Jill — let's go back inside. We can take some of those cartons of books up to the third floor. Unless you're tired, that is. I don't want to wear you out or anything."

Jill scrambled to her feet. "Don't be silly! I love helping you get settled in your new room. It's much bigger and nicer than your old one. And you have your very own bathroom, too."

They climbed down the ladder to the ground, Cleveland complaining all the way. As they headed for the back porch, Val said, "We haven't fixed up the bathroom yet. The shower doesn't work right and the toilet makes funny noises when you flush it. But Dad called the plumber and he's coming on Wednesday. It won't be my private bathroom — with six people in the house, I'll have to share, but that's okay."

She opened the back door just wide enough to let herself and Jill in without letting the two dogs out. Jocko, the little black-and-white mongrel, and Andy, the big tan mixed breed, greeted the girls with happy barks and wagging tails. Cleveland leaped from Val's shoulder to the kitchen counter and began to wash.

With the dogs scampering at their heels, Val and Jill went upstairs to Val's room on the second floor. They each picked up a carton of books and carried them up another flight to her new bedroom. Doc had moved her bookshelves last week, after they had finished painting the walls a sky-blue. Val's desk and her chair were there, too.

"I do my homework here now," she told Jill. "I can't wait till we move the rest of my furniture. Dad says we'll probably do that next week. Then we'll start redecorating my old room for Sparky."

"I bet I know what she wants," Jill said as she started placing books on the shelves. "Wallpaper with spaceman and androids, right?"

Val grinned. "You got it. But Catherine thinks she should have something like flowers. Hey, Jill, your mother's a decorator. Do you think she could find a wallpaper that has spacemen and androids *and* flowers?"

They both laughed. "Somehow I doubt it," Jill said.

"So do I!" Val glanced at her watch. "Gee, it's almost four o'clock. Dad's been over at Catherine's house for hours, talking about the wedding. I wonder if they've made up their minds!"

Peering out the window, Jill said, "Well, we'll find out in a few minutes. Your father's car just pulled into the driveway!"

Chapter
4

Val, Jill, Andy, and Jocko dashed down the stairs and reached the entrance hall just as Doc and Teddy came in the front door. A moment later, Erin arrived. She had been visiting her friend Olivia, rehearsing for the spring recital of Miss Tamara's Ballet School.

"Cookies!" Teddy shouted, charging toward the kitchen. "Me and Sparky and the gang have been playing softball, and I'm starvin' like Marvin!" Jocko galloped after him.

Erin took Doc's hand and pulled him into the living room. "Daddy, what did you and Catherine decide? Please tell us — I'm dying to know!" Andy jumped up and down as though he were as eager to find out as Erin was.

"Yes, Dad. What are you going to do?" Val asked. She and Jill followed her father, Erin, and Andy.

Doc sat down in his favorite chair next to the fireplace. *"Down*, Andy," he said. "Ladies, let me catch my breath."

Val and Jill dropped onto the sofa, while Erin sat on the floor at her father's feet. They all looked at him expectantly, and Andy let out an excited *"Woof!"*

"They're gonna get married right here!" Teddy said as he came into the room with a tin of Mrs. Racer's oatmeal-raisin-nut cookies. "And Judge Gross is gonna marry them, and it's all settled, isn't it, Dad?"

"You mean you're not going to have a big, fancy wedding after all?" Erin asked. "I won't be able to wear my toe shoes, and Miss Maggie's garden will go to waste?" She looked so disappointed that Doc reached out and stroked her sleek, silvery-blonde head.

"Yes and no, honey," he said. "We are *not* going to be married in town hall, but if you want to wear your toe shoes here, that's perfectly okay. And Miss Maggie's garden won't go to waste. Catherine and I have decided that after a very small, simple wedding here on Old Mill Road, we'll have the reception on Miss Maggie's estate. That way everyone who isn't invited to the ceremony will at least be able to participate in the celebration afterward and nobody will be left out."

"Dad phoned Mayor Anderson," Teddy added, passing the tin of cookies around, "and he thinks it's a great idea."

"So do I," Val said, beaming. She grabbed a handful of cookies and gave some to Jill.

Jill nodded. "Me, too." Then she glanced shyly at Doc. "Uh . . . if it's a *very* small wedding, I guess that means my folks and I aren't invited, right?"

"Of course you are!" Val cried. "Dad, Jill and her parents can come, can't they?"

"Indeed they may," Doc said. "Catherine and I made up two guest lists, one for the wedding and one for the reception. The first includes only the people who work at Animal Inn — including Donna's husband, Jim, of course — the Dearbornes, Mrs. Racer and her son, Henry, Catherine's housekeeper Mrs. Wilson and her husband, and of course Miss Maggie."

"Oh, good!" Jill bounded off the sofa and headed for the door. "Tell Catherine not to waste a stamp — I'm going right home to tell my parents myself. 'Bye, Val. See you in school tomorrow!"

As she ran out the door, Val said, "Does Miss Maggie know what you've decided, Dad?"

"She probably does by now," Doc replied. "Catherine was trying to reach her when I left. She's also going to suggest that Mrs. Wilson and Mrs. Racer might be willing to help Miss Maggie prepare the food."

"Daddy . . ." Erin said thoughtfully, "you're asking thirteen people to the wedding, right?"

Munching on a cookie, Doc nodded.

"Well, thirteen's an unlucky number, and I think it's a bad idea for you and Catherine to start your married life that way," Erin went on. "Now, if you invited my best friend Olivia and her parents, that would make it sixteen.''

''Hey, yeah, Dad! And how about asking Eric and Billy?'' Teddy put in. '' 'Cause if you're inviting Vallie's best friend and Erin's best friend, it's not fair if you don't invite *my* best friends, too!''

''Whoa!'' Doc held up both hands. ''We're inviting the Dearbornes because Jill is practically a member of the family. As for the rest of our friends, they can all come to the reception.'' He turned to Erin. ''And don't worry about an 'unlucky' number, honey. Counting the wedding party and Judge Gross, that makes twenty, which is the luckiest number of all.''

Erin looked surprised. ''It is? I never knew that.''

''Few people do, because I just made it up,'' Doc told her with a grin. ''But I know what I'm talking about, because I'm a very lucky man!''

Everyone was glad when Miss Maggie agreed that a small ceremony at the Taylors' house was a sensible idea. Catherine and Doc tried to convince her to let them share the cost of the reception, but she wouldn't hear of it. This was to be her wedding gift to them, and as the old lady had pointed out earlier, she could well afford it.

''I quite understand why you're insisting on no presents from your guests, but surely you can make an exception in my case,'' Miss Maggie said. And since Miss Maggie was always the exception to every rule, Doc and Catherine gave in. But she didn't object to Mrs. Racer and Mrs. Wilson preparing some of the food, which made both women very happy.

The news of the wedding arrangements traveled even faster than usual. On Monday, Lila Bascombe joined Val, Jill, and several of their friends at the table where they were having lunch in the Hamilton cafeteria. Taking an empty seat next to Val, Lila said with a big smile, "I think it's so clever of your father and Mrs. Sparks to talk Great-aunt Maggie into hosting their wedding reception!"

Before Val could retort angrily that the whole thing had been Miss Maggie's idea, Lila went on, "My mother says it's going to be *the* social event of the year, and everybody who *is* anybody will be invited."

"She's absolutely right," Jill said sweetly as Val fumed. "But they're making an exception in your case, Lila. *You're* going to be invited, too!"

Val, Sarah, Lisa, and Nancy snorted with laughter, but Lila didn't seem to realize she'd been insulted. She just kept babbling merrily away. "Of course, it won't be nearly as *exclusive* as the Horse Show Ball in July. It's going to be held at Longmeadow Farm, the Merrills' estate, and nobody but exhibitors will receive invitations. I happen to know all about it, because Mummy is on the social committee." She took a dainty bite of her sloppy joe. "Too bad your old horse won't be able to compete, Val. You'll miss all the fun."

"Oh, I don't know about that," Val heard herself say. "The Ghost isn't really all that old, and he's going to have an operation very soon that will remove the cataracts in his eyes. As a matter of fact, I'm planning on entering him in the show."

Jill stared at her. "You are? That's terrific! Why didn't you tell me?"

"I just didn't get around to it, I guess," Val mumbled, poking at her meatless taco salad with her fork. She wished she hadn't said anything, but the words had just popped out and now she couldn't take them back.

"Gee, Val, that's great!" Sarah said. "Are you going to ride him?"

Val raised her head and stuck out her chin. "Yes, I am. I'm going to prove that The Ghost is still the champion he used to be!"

Lila's eyebrows shot up. "Really? Is your father going to operate on him?"

"No," Val said. "But he knows a specialist in Philadelphia who can do it. Dad's going to make the arrangements tomorrow."

"A specialist?" Lila was impressed. "That sounds very expensive. Specialists charge hundreds and *hundreds* of dollars! How can you possibly afford it?"

Gritting her teeth, Val replied, "I've been saving my money ever since I got The Ghost, that's how. And I earned it, every cent!"

"Well, if you're really riding in the show, I guess

I'll have to tell Mummy to add your name to the invitation list for the ball." Lila sighed.

"Don't bother," Val snapped. "I don't care about that at all. But I *do* care about The Ghost. When he can see the way he used to, he'll be happy and so will I."

"You know what, Val?" said Nancy eagerly. "The Ghost's comeback would make a fantastic story for the *Essex Gazette*. I can see the headline now — 'Local Teenager's Champion Jumper Wins Again!' "

Lila frowned. "Why would the *Gazette* want to print something like that? They weren't interested when my poodle, Marie Antoinette, won a blue ribbon at the dog show last fall."

"That's because Toni isn't famous the way The Ghost used to be," Lisa told her. "It's not the same thing at all."

Lila had finished her lunch and now she stood and picked up her tray. "Maybe not, but nobody's going to be interested unless he wins," she said with a smug little smile. "And he hasn't even had that operation yet. Until he does, he's still nothing but an old, blind horse!"

Val glared after her as Lila marched off, and Jill patted her shoulder. "Don't pay any attention to Lila," she said. "She's just jealous. You know that she can't stand the thought of anybody being more important than she is."

"That's for sure," Nancy added. "And if she's jealous now, imagine how green she's going to be when The Ghost actually *does* win!"

Val could imagine it, all right, and the picture of Lila pea-green with envy made her grin. But much as she hated to admit it to herself, what Lila had said was partly true. If the surgery failed to restore The Ghost's sight, he couldn't compete in the show at all, and Lila wouldn't hesitate to say "I told you so." Again Val wished she hadn't revealed her secret plan. But she had, and that was that. . . .

"Earth to Val! Earth to Val! Come in, please," she heard Jill saying and realized that her friend had just asked her a question.

"Sorry — what did you say?" she asked.

"I *said*, What does The Ghost think about all this?" Jill repeated. "You have to understand that Val's a little weird," she said to the other girls. "She has conversations with animals just as if they were people!"

"What's so weird about that?" Sarah asked. "I talk to my dog all the time, and he talks back. He even knows how to say my brother's name — every time he barks, he goes 'Ralph! Ralph! Ralph!' "

Laughing, Val said, "Thanks, Sarah." Turning back to Jill, she added, "For your information, Miss Dearborne, I haven't told him yet. But I'm going to tell him this afternoon, so there!"

Jill giggled. "I can't wait to hear what he has to say."

* * *

As soon as school was over for the day, Val biked out to Animal Inn. Since the clinic was closed on Mondays, it was one of the few times during the week when she could ride her horse for as long as she liked.

After stopping by the Small Animal Clinic to say hello to Mike Strickler, Val headed for The Ghost's pasture behind the barn. Instead of trotting over to her, tossing his head, and whickering a greeting at the sound of her voice as he used to, the dapple-gray gelding plodded slowly to her side.

"Oh, Ghost, cheer up," Val said softly as she threw her arms around his glossy neck. "I brought some carrots for you, and then we're going for a nice long ride."

The Ghost's ears pricked up at the sight of the carrots, and he munched them contentedly while Val led him back to the barn.

"I have some real exciting news for you," Val told her horse as she brushed his coat and combed his silvery mane. "Something wonderful is going to happen! You're going to have an operation so you can see again, and then you'll be able to jump again, too!"

The Ghost looked mildly interested, and Val continued, "I'm going to start taking riding lessons next week. I want to learn as much as I can so I can ride you in the horse show. I wouldn't want to fall off or anything — Lila would laugh herself sick if I did, and so would that awful Cassandra Merrill! Oh,

Ghost, it's going to be fabulous! You and me, flying over the jumps just like in that dream I had when I first got you. Only in the dream, you really *were* flying. You were Pegasus, the winged horse, and I was riding you bareback."

Val hurried off to get The Ghost's saddle and bridle. "Of course, I couldn't do that in real life," she said when she returned and began saddling him. "Even if I was good enough by the beginning of July, I don't think you're allowed to ride bareback in a jumping class. But still, it'll be a dream come true, my dream and yours."

She fastened the throat latch of his bridle, then led The Ghost out of his stall and sprang into the saddle. "Just imagine, Ghost," Val sighed as he gently jog-trotted out of the barn. "By this time next month, I'll have a stepmother and a stepsister, and if Dr. Weintraub can perform the surgery very soon, maybe you'll be able to see clearly again."

If. Maybe, echoed a persistent little voice inside her head. *Remember what your father said. The operation is very risky. If it fails, The Ghost could be totally blind. Totally blind. Totally blind. Maybe you ought to reconsider. . . .*

"No!" Val said aloud, so sharply that her horse flicked his ears in surprise. She patted his satiny shoulder. "Sorry, Ghost. I didn't mean to startle you," she told him. "The surgery *will* succeed, I'm sure it will. And then everybody will know you're still a champion!"

Chapter
5

It seemed to Val that Tuesday had more than the normal number of hours in it. As the day dragged on, all she could think of was the fact that while she was sitting in class, or playing volleyball in gym, or picking at her lunch in the cafeteria, Doc might be speaking to Dr. Weintraub and arranging for The Ghost's operation. When was the earliest he could perform the surgery? she wondered. Would Doc let her go with him when he took The Ghost to Dr. Weintraub's clinic? Animal Inn didn't have a horse van. Who could they borrow one from? How long would it take for The Ghost's eyes to heal so he could begin jumping again?

Before her afternoon classes began, Val got permission to use the pay phone in the office and called Animal Inn. But Pat Dempwolf, Doc's receptionist, said that Doc was busy with a patient, and no, she didn't know if he'd spoken to somebody named Aaron Weintraub. "Why do you want to know, Val-lie?" Pat asked. "Is anything wrong?"

"No, nothing's wrong. See you later, Pat. Gotta run!" Val hung up and trudged down the hall to her English class. Only two more hours to go, and then she'd have the answers to at least some of her questions.

The minute she arrived at Animal Inn, Val dashed off in search of her father. She found him in his private office, writing up a chart on one of his patients. As she put on a clean white lab coat over her T-shirt and jeans, she said eagerly, "Did you talk to him, Dad? What did he say? When can Dr. Weintraub operate on The Ghost's eyes?"

Doc put down his clipboard and smiled at her. But it was what Val thought of as his "serious" smile, and it usually meant that he wasn't very happy about what he was thinking. She felt a tight little knot begin to form in her stomach.

"Yes, I spoke to him," Doc said. "But I'm afraid you're not going to like what he had to say."

The little knot got even tighter. "What do you mean?" Val asked, sitting on the edge of the chair across the desk from him. "Won't he perform the surgery?"

Doc leaned back in his chair. "That's not the problem, Vallie. Though he mentioned the things you and I have already discussed — The Ghost's age, the risk of blindness if the operation doesn't succeed — he brought up another point that neither of us had considered, and that's the cost."

"But we *have* considered it!" Val exclaimed. "I told you I've saved up a thousand dollars, and that's not even counting the interest my money's earned. The way I figure it is that because he's a specialist, Dr. Weintraub probably charges around twice what you do for an operation, and the most you've ever charged is four hundred dollars. And that means that I can pay his fee and have money left over for . . ." Val didn't want to mention the wedding present she intended to buy, so she finished by saying, ". . . for other things."

Doc rubbed his beard. "Honey, let me explain something to you. I'm a small-town vet with a rural practice. I charge for my services what I think my clients can afford."

Val smiled slightly. "Yes, I know. And sometimes you don't charge them anything at all if you know they don't have much money."

"That's right. Well, that's not the way Dr. Weintraub does business. His clinic is very well known, not just in Pennsylvania, but all over the country. And his clients are very wealthy. Their horses are very valuable, so they're willing to pay a great deal to protect their investments. . . ."

"How much?" Val asked.

"A thousand dollars for the surgery," Doc said.

Val felt the knot in her stomach relax. "Whew! It's okay then! I can handle it. I won't have anything left over to spend on what I was going to spend it on, but that's okay, too. I'll just take fewer riding lessons."

"There's more," Doc told her. "After the surgery, The Ghost will have to stay at Dr. Weintraub's clinic for several weeks so he and his staff can monitor The Ghost's progress as he recuperates."

Val swallowed hard. "How much?" she asked again.

"A minimum of another thousand," Doc replied.

"Another thousand?" Val gasped. "Oh, Dad, it'll take me another *year* to save up that much money! That's awful! And The Ghost will be another year older, and that means there'll be even less chance of the surgery succeeding. He needs the operation *now*!"

"Doc, I hate to interrupt you, but there are a lot of patients waiting out here, and their owners are wondering where you are," Pat's voice squawked over the intercom. "Are you coming out soon?"

Doc pressed the button and said, "Yes, Pat. Be there in a minute." He turned back to Val. "Honey, we have work to do. Let's discuss this later, when office hours are over, okay?"

Val nodded miserably. "Sure. Whatever you say."

Her father came around the desk and touched her cheek. "I'm sorry, Vallie. It never occurred to me how expensive this might be." He smiled ruefully. "Maybe you ought to rethink coming into practice with me when you graduate from vet school. You could do a lot better financially as a specialist."

Val stood up and put her arms around him. "I don't care about that! I want to be the kind of vet you are right here in Essex, where everybody says 'God bless you' every time someone sneezes!"

Doc threw back his head and laughed. "Good girl!" He released her and headed for the door. "I'll be in the first treatment room. Bring in the next patient, please."

Two thousand dollars, Val kept repeating to herself as she went into the reception area and took the leash of McTavish, a bouncy black-and-white Border collie. McTavish's owner, an attractive young woman holding a little boy by the hand, said, "Excuse me, Miss, but could you give me some idea of how much my dog's checkup is going to cost? We're new in town, and this is our first visit to Dr. Taylor."

"Two thousand dollars," Val said automatically.

The young woman's face paled. *"Two thou — "*

Realizing what she had just said, Val exclaimed, "No! No, I was only kidding. I was thinking about something else. It won't be more than twenty-five. Check with Pat — she's the lady behind the desk. Come on, McTavish. Let's go see my dad."

She hurried out of the waiting room and almost bumped into Toby, who was standing in the hall by the open door. "Are you nuts?" he whispered. "Why did you tell that woman it would cost her two thousand dollars for a checkup?"

"I made a mistake," Val mumbled. "Like I said, I was thinking about something else, something that *will* cost that much money. And I don't know how I'm going to pay for it."

Toby walked beside her to the first treatment room. "You're not gonna buy Doc and Catherine a real expensive wedding present, are you?" he asked. "I mean, I know you want to get them something special, but . . ."

Val shook her head. "No, that's not it. I'll tell you about it later, after I've helped Dad take care of McTavish."

But after McTavish's checkup, Doc needed Val's help with several other patients. It was almost an hour later when Val joined Toby in the infirmary where he was getting the afternoon medications ready.

"So what's up?" Toby asked, and Val told him all about the horse show, her plan to restore The Ghost's sight, and Doc's conversation with Dr. Weintraub. When she had finished, he said, "Wow! That's a lot of money to spend on a horse you bought for two hundred dollars!"

"That's not the point," Val said impatiently. "The Ghost is worth every penny of it, but I don't have it. And I can't possibly save up another thousand until some time next year."

Toby opened one of the cages, lifted out a skinny calico cat, and popped two pills down her throat. "Maybe you could get a loan," he suggested. "That's what your dad did when he wanted to build the boarding kennel and he didn't have enough money."

For a moment, Val brightened. "Hey, that's not a bad idea!" Then she sighed. "But it won't work. No bank is going to lend a thousand dollars to a thirteen-year-old kid." She gently rubbed some antibiotic ointment on the sores around a Siberian husky's mouth, patted him, and put him back into his cage.

"Yeah, you're probably right," Toby agreed. "Uh . . . Val, I have a couple of hundred saved up. If it would help, you could borrow it. For a little while, anyway."

Val was touched by Toby's offer. She knew that he was saving to buy a motorbike he'd been wanting for a long time. "Thanks, Toby," she said, smiling. "It's really nice of you, but I can't take your money. I'll just have to think of some way to come up with the other thousand on my own."

She and Toby took care of a few more sick or injured pets. Then Toby said suddenly, "Why?"

Val blinked. "Why what? What are you talking about?"

"Why do you want to spend all that money on an operation that might leave The Ghost worse off than he is now?"

"Haven't you been listening to me?" Val asked,

exasperated. "I want him to have the surgery because if there's even the tiniest chance he'll be able to see and jump again, he deserves it. You've seen the way The Ghost has been acting lately, all droopy and listless. I'm sure it's because he misses being able to jump. He's like — like a bird that can't fly! And when I enter him in the horse show, Cassandra Merrill will be sorry she gave up on him so easily!"

Toby's ears began to turn pink. "You don't have to yell at me, Val. Look at it this way — maybe The Ghost can't jump now, but he can still see a little. If he were my horse, I don't think I'd want to take the risk of him not being able to see at all just because I wanted to show off for the Merrills."

Val slammed the door of the last cage. "I can't believe you said that, Toby Curran! That's *not* the reason I want him to have the operation! It's for *his* sake, not mine!"

Toby shrugged. "Have it your own way. But if you really care about him so much, I guess I don't understand why you can't just leave him be."

"You don't understand, all right!" Val shouted. "You don't understand *anything*! I'm sorry I even told you about it!" She shoved the medication cart into a corner and stamped out of the infirmary, calling over her shoulder, "And I am *not* a show-off, so there!"

Val was still angry when she and Doc got into the Animal Inn van at the end of the day. As he backed the van out of the parking lot, Doc glanced over at her and asked, "Something wrong, Vallie?"

"You bet there is!" Val folded her arms across her chest and scowled. "Do you know what Toby had the nerve to say to me?"

"No, but I have a feeling I'm about to find out," her father said, turning the van onto Schoolhouse Lane.

"He actually said that the real reason I want The Ghost to have the operation and enter the jumping competition is because I want to show off for the Merrills! And he said that if I really cared about him, I wouldn't try to save his sight! For somebody who's supposed to be my friend, Toby sure doesn't act like one!"

"I see," Doc said. After a brief silence, he went on, "You know something, honey? Just because somebody tells you something you don't want to hear doesn't mean he's not your friend."

Val stared at him. "You mean you *agree* with him? *You* think I'm a show-off, too?"

Doc reached out and patted her knee. "No, Vallie, I don't think that. I know how much you love The Ghost, and how much his happiness and well-being mean to you. As a matter of fact, I've been thinking about how we can handle the cost of the operation, and I have a proposition for you."

Val's anger quickly faded. "Oh, Dad, really? What is it?" she asked eagerly.

"Well, I'd be willing to lend you the rest of the money you need — "

"Oh, Dad!" Val cried again. "That's terrific! I'll pay you back, every cent, honest!"

" — but there are strings attached," Doc continued. "First of all, I want you to think very long and hard about the risks involved. And second, I want you to think about what Toby said to you today."

"But . . . but . . . but . . ." Val spluttered.

"Let me finish," Doc said quietly. "I know you're not a show-off in the usual sense, somebody who brags a lot and acts like she's better than everybody else."

"Like Lila Bascombe," Val put in, frowning. "I can't wait to see her face when — " she glanced over at her father — "*if* The Ghost wins a blue ribbon in the horse show."

"That's exactly what I mean," Doc said. "You want to put Lila and the Merrills in their place, which is perfectly understandable. But I want you to consider very, very carefully what's more important — The Ghost's welfare, or the possibility of scoring a triumph over some people you don't particularly like."

Val scrunched down in her seat, biting her lower lip. Finally she said, "When you put it that way, I don't really have much choice, do I?"

"Yes, you do," Doc told her. "Because there *is* a chance, though it's a very slim one, that Dr. Weintraub may be able to remove The Ghost's cataracts and your horse will be able to jump again. On the other hand, if the surgery fails, he may lose what little sight he has."

"But if we don't try, we'll never know," Val murmured. Then she sighed. "If only horses could talk! Jill makes fun of me because I talk to animals all the time. But they never answer back, not even The Ghost. If they did, I could ask him what he wants me to do."

Doc steered the van onto Old Mill Road. "That would be nice, wouldn't it?" he said, smiling. "I've often wished that my patients could tell me exactly where it hurts so I wouldn't have to rely on what their owners have to say. Unfortunately they can't, so I have to make my own decisions based on the evidence I'm presented with. And so do you. We're the guardians of the animals committed to our care, and we have to do our best to make sure we do what's right for them."

As the van pulled into the driveway next to the Taylors' house, Val turned to her father. "Dad, what do *you* think I should do?"

Brushing a strand of chestnut-brown hair from her cheek, Doc said, "Honey, The Ghost is your horse. The decision is up to you. If you're going to be a vet, you'll have to make decisions like this every day. And believe me, it's never easy."

"But what if I make the wrong choice?" Val said softly.

"You won't." Doc unbuckled his seat belt and got out of the van. "Coming?"

Val nodded. Unfastening her seat belt, too, she got out and helped Doc take her bike from the back of the van. After she wheeled it into the garage, she followed her father up the path to the back porch.

Before he opened the kitchen door, Doc looked down at her and said, "You don't have to make up your mind right away, Vallie. In fact, I'd rather you didn't. Take your time. Dr. Weintraub wouldn't be able to schedule the surgery for several weeks. Give it a lot of thought."

"I will," Val assured him. "I probably won't be able to think about anything else!"

Chapter 6

But though Val thought and thought, by the end of the week she still hadn't decided what to do about The Ghost. And she hadn't decided on a wedding present for her father and Catherine, either.

On Friday after school, Jill marched her down to Main Street and dragged her from store to store, pointing out various possibilities.

"You can't just let it go until the last minute," Jill said, stopping in front of Reineman's jewelry store. "Look at that lovely china vase, the cream-colored one with the gold trim. Catherine likes flowers — I bet she'd love something like that. Vases are very useful. My mother has dozens of them."

"So do we," Val sighed. "And Catherine probably does, too. I want to give them something really special, something they don't already have." Thinking about her conversation with Toby back when they were still good friends, she added, "It ought to be something they can share. Somehow I don't think they'd enjoy arranging flowers together."

Jill giggled. "I guess you're right. Okay, how about those silver goblets? They're pretty expensive, but you don't have to buy the whole set. You could just get two, one for Doc and one for Catherine. They could drink champagne out of them on their wedding day."

"Yeah, and then they'd never use them again," Val pointed out. "They'd just sit on a shelf and get all tarnished."

Jill's patience was wearing thin. "Okay, forget the vase and forget the goblets. What about that porcelain figure of a bird sitting on a branch? Isn't it beautiful? And it looks so real!"

Val glanced at the figurine without much interest. "It's pretty, but the cats would probably knock it over and break it."

"I give up!" Jill groaned. "At this rate, you'll be lucky to decide on a present by their first anniversary!"

"I'm sorry, Jill," Val said. "I know you're trying to help, but what I want is . . ."

". . . something really special?" Jill finished for her. "I know. But I'm beginning to think that whatever it is, you're not going to find it here in Essex."

"I'm beginning to think so, too," Val admitted as she and Jill walked away from the jewelry store. "I can't seem to make up my mind about anything these days, not even The Ghost's operation."

Jill looked surprised. "I thought that was all settled. On Monday you said your father was making the arrangements."

"Well, he spoke to Dr. Weintraub, but he left it up to me to decide whether to go through with it or not."

"Why wouldn't you want to go through with it?" Jill asked, puzzled. "Don't you want to ride The Ghost in the horse show and prove he's still a champion?"

"Of course I do, but it's not as simple as all that." After Val explained the risks involved in the surgery and the amount of money it would cost, Jill said, "If you want my opinion, I think you should go for it. The Ghost isn't happy the way he is now. It wouldn't be fair to deny him the chance to see again, even if it's a very small chance."

"That's exactly what I think — half the time, anyway," Val said. "But the rest of the time, I'm just not sure. Toby and I had a big fight about it the other day."

"Again?" Jill rolled her eyes. "You guys are always arguing about something! It's a wonder you're still friends."

"We're not," Val snapped. "We've hardly spoken to each other all week. *He* thinks I care more about showing off for the Merrills and Lila Bascombe than I do about The Ghost! Toby says if I really cared about my horse, I'd leave well enough alone." She stared down at the sidewalk, murmuring, "And the worst part of it is that sometimes I think maybe he's right. I just don't know what to do!"

"I've got a great idea!" Jill said cheerfully, stopping in front of Kane's Kandy Store. "It won't help solve your problem, but if you're as thirsty as I am, it'll make you feel better. Let's go into Kane's and order a couple of ice cream sodas. Then you can come over to my house, and we can play some video games."

The thought appealed to Val, but she shook her head. "I can't. I promised Mrs. Racer I'd be home in time to try on my bridesmaid's dress before she leaves tonight. She's basted the skirt to the top but she doesn't want to sew it on the machine until she's sure it fits."

"Neat! That sounds like much more fun," Jill said. "Can I come along and see how it looks? I really don't have to be home until six, and I'd love to see you in a dress for a change!"

Val couldn't help grinning. "Come on, Jill! You saw me in a dress at Miss Maggie's Christmas party."

"Right — almost five months ago!" Jill laughed. "I've forgotten what you looked like. Can I come?"

Val shrugged. "Sure — why not?"

The two girls turned around and started back down Main Street. "What are you going to wear to the wedding, or don't you know yet?" Val asked.

"Of course I do!" Jill said. "You know me — I always plan everything in advance. Mom and I went to the mall the other night, and I found this really adorable dress. It's pale lavender with little blue flowers sprinkled all over it, and ruffles at the neck and sleeves. When I wear it, I feel like Scarlett O'Hara in *Gone with the Wind*. What's Catherine going to wear?"

"I don't know. I don't think she knows, either. She hasn't had much time to shop, what with her job and all. But it's not going to be a fancy white gown with a veil or anything."

"I saw this dress in one of Mom's magazines that I think would be just perfect for Catherine," Jill said. "It's kind of an off-white silk brocade with long sleeves and it's very tailored, like a shirtwaist only dressier, if you know what I mean. And Mom said they have the exact same thing in Brenda's Boutique! You ought to tell Catherine to check it out."

"Okay, I will."

Val was happy to talk about clothes because it kept her from thinking about the decisions she had to make. But if she didn't make up her mind soon about The Ghost, it might be too late for him to recover from the surgery in time to compete in the horse show.

When Val and Jill came into the Taylors' house, they found Mrs. Racer bending over the sewing machine on the dining room table.

"Hello, Vallie," she said, glancing up from the seam she was stitching. In her simple dress and the little white lawn cap perched on the back of her snowy head, Val thought she looked just like an illustration from a book about the Mennonites, the "Plain People" who lived and worked in Central Pennsylvania. "Afternoon, Jill. Did you come to see the fashion show?"

"That's right." Jill went over to the dress hanging from the door frame between the dining room and the kitchen. "Oh, Mrs. Racer, this is really gorgeous!" she cried, fingering the rose-pink and sage-green print fabric. "Is this Val's dress?"

Mrs. Racer nodded as she fed the last of the flowered material under the presser foot of the sewing machine. "Sure is. And I'm finishing the bodice of Erin's right now. I figure it ought to be ready for her to try on by tomorrow. Then I'll start on Sparky's."

"Come on, Val. Take off those ratty jeans and that droopy T-shirt," Jill said eagerly. "I can't wait to see how you look in this beautiful dress!"

Val obediently went into the kitchen and shucked off her clothes. Jill helped her get into the bridesmaid's dress, fluffing up the puffed sleeves and smoothing the gathers of the full skirt. When she had zipped up the back, she stood back to admire the effect.

"You look absolutely fantastic," she cried. "Or you will, when your hair's fixed. And those sneakers and socks have to go. What are you going to wear on your feet for the wedding?"

"My feet?" Val repeated. "Gee, I hadn't thought about that. I guess I'll wear my black patent leather flats with the bows on the toes. They're the only dressy shoes I've got."

Jill shook her head. "No way! You can't wear black to a wedding — it's bad luck."

"That's right, Vallie," Mrs. Racer called from the dining room. " 'Married in black, wish you were back.' "

"But *I'm* not the one who's getting married," Val pointed out.

"It doesn't matter," Jill said firmly. "You and Erin and Sparky have to wear shoes that coordinate with your dresses. Let's see . . ." She peered at Val through narrowed eyes. "I think you all ought to get white satin or linen shoes and have them dyed to match. Sparky and Erin can wear flats, and you should wear pumps."

Val curled her toes inside her comfortable old sneakers. "You mean with heels? I've never worn heels in my life! I'll probably trip or something. And besides, I'm five eight in my stocking feet. I'll look like a giant in heels."

Giggling, Jill grabbed her hand and pulled her into the dining room. "You will not. Now come show Mrs. Racer how perfectly your dress fits."

When Mrs. Racer saw Val, she said softly, "Oh, Vallie, you look just like a princess in one of them fairy tale books!" She dabbed at her eyes with a corner of her apron. "You're getting so grown-up. Seems like yesterday you were just a toddler running around the house . . ." She gave herself a little shake, then said in her usual brisk voice, "Let me take a closer look. I think it's a little short-waisted. And how do the armholes feel? Not too tight, are they?"

Val flapped her arms and wiggled her shoulders. "Nope. Everything feels just . . ."

"*Yeeeooow!*"

Val, Jill, and Mrs. Racer jumped as a gray-and-white blur shot through the kitchen doorway, followed closely by an orange blur. Cleveland was in hot pursuit of Sparky's cat, Charlie, and they were both screeching at the top of their lungs.

"My stars!" Mrs. Racer gasped.

"What's Charlie doing here?" Val asked in astonishment as Charlie rounded the dining room table, leaped onto a chair, and from there to the top of the china cabinet, hissing and spitting. She lunged for Cleveland, and as she grabbed her cat around his fat, furry middle, she heard a ripping sound.

"Oh, no," she wailed. "Mrs. Racer, I think something just tore!"

"Cleveland! Bad cat!" Erin, in leotard and tights, dashed into the room with Sparky at her heels. "You're supposed to be making friends with Charlie, not scaring him to death!"

"Yeah, Cleveland," Sparky added, scowling at the big orange cat struggling in Val's arms. "That's why I brought him over today, so you could get to know each other." Her round little face was worried as she looked around. "Where *is* Charlie, anyway?"

"Up there." Jill pointed to the china cabinet

where Charlie sat. His fur was standing on end, and he was lashing his tail angrily.

Val really looked at Sparky for the first time, and when she did, it was all she could do not to burst out laughing. Instead of the jeans and T-shirt Sparky usually wore, she had on one of Erin's ballet costumes. Val remembered the pale blue tutu from Miss Tamara's recital a few years ago, and though it was much too small for Erin now, it was still too large for Sparky. The tulle skirt dropped almost to the little girl's plump knees, and the sequined straps kept slipping off her shoulders.

Chewing on the end of one stubby pigtail, Sparky stared up at Charlie. "Cleveland didn't hurt you, did he?" she asked anxiously. "Are you okay?"

"Wrrowoowow," Charlie muttered and began to wash.

Val put Cleveland in the kitchen and closed the door behind her as she returned. "He looks fine to me," she said. "He was moving too fast for Cleveland to lay a claw on him. Just leave him alone, Sparky. He'll come down when he's good and ready."

Jill caught her eye, and Val could tell that her friend was trying as hard as she was not to laugh. "Uh . . . Sparky," Jill said, "that's some outfit you're wearing. Are you in a play or something?"

The little girl shook her head. Around the end of her pigtail, she mumbled, "Huh-uh. Erin's teaching me to be a ballet dancer just like her."

"Yes, I am," Erin said, beaming. "I'm giving

Sparky lessons so she'll have a head start when she enters Miss Tamara's class in the fall."

"Now isn't that nice!" Mrs. Racer said. She gave Sparky a hug, and removed the pigtail from her mouth. "I bet you're both hungry, aren't you? You've been working real hard, I can tell. How about some cookies and milk?"

"All right!" Sparky grinned. She trotted after Erin toward the kitchen, then stopped and turned back. Looking from Mrs. Racer to Val and Jill, she said, "It's kind of a secret — the ballet lessons, I mean. Don't tell Teddy, okay? 'Cause if he finds out, he'll laugh at me and then I'll have to beat him up."

Very solemnly, Val said, "We won't say a word, honest."

"Cross your heart and hope to die?" Sparky asked.

"You got it," Jill assured her.

When the kitchen door had closed behind Sparky and Erin, Val and Jill clapped their hands over their mouths to stifle their laughter.

"I can't *believe* it!" Jill giggled. "Sparky wants to be a ballet dancer! Things sure are changing around here!"

"Speaking of changing, can I change into my regular clothes now?" Val asked Mrs. Racer. "I'm sorry about the rip. I didn't ruin the dress or anything, did I?"

Examining the fabric around the armholes, Mrs. Racer shook her white head. "No, it was just a seam.

I can stitch it up real easy. Maybe I ought to bring a needle and thread to the wedding, in case you decide to go chasing after some other animal!"

"I won't," Val promised. "I'll be so ladylike you won't recognize me."

The old lady smiled at her affectionately. "I don't know as I'd like that, Vallie. I think you're pretty special exactly the way you are!"

Chapter 7

Val's first riding lesson was scheduled for two o'clock on Sunday afternoon. Paula Morgan's stable was several miles outside of town, and as Val rode her bike along Accomac Road, she wondered what her teacher would be like. She had been surprised to discover that Doc didn't know her and had never treated any of her horses. Val figured that meant either Ms. Morgan's horses were unusually healthy, or her vet was Dr. Callahan over in Harrisburg.

"Aren't you kind of putting the cart before the horse, honey?" Doc asked when Val told him about her appointment. "It seems to me it would make more sense to decide what you're going to do about The Ghost before you start learning to ride him in the show. And you haven't made up your mind yet, have you?"

"No," Val admitted, "not quite. I'm almost positive I want him to have the operation — today, anyway. Who knows what I'll think tomorrow? But either way, I want to learn to be a better rider because The

Ghost deserves the best of everything."

Doc offered to drive her to Ms. Morgan's place, but Val said she'd bike instead. She knew that her father planned to spend the day with Teddy, painting the woodwork in her old bedroom, and she didn't want to take him away from his work.

Now Val saw an old red barn up ahead on the left side of the road. Ms. Morgan had told her on the phone that just beyond the barn was Walnut Lane where she was to make a right. As Val did, she saw a sign that read MORGAN'S — RIDING INSTRUCTION AND BOARDING.

She passed gently rolling pastures where sleek horses grazed, and soon she caught sight of a low, white barn. As Val approached, she saw a child who looked to be about Erin's age taking a sorrel horse over a series of jumps in a ring to one side of the barn. Val couldn't tell if the rider was a boy or a girl because of the velvet riding helmet the child was wearing. It looked so effortless and easy! Her heart began to beat faster. In just a few minutes, she would be taking the first real step toward making her dream come true! Slowing her bike to a stop in front of the barn, Val decided then and there that as soon as she got home, she would ask Doc to call Dr. Weintraub again and set up a definite appointment for The Ghost's surgery.

When she got off her bike, Val looked around. The only person she saw was the kid in the jumping ring. Not quite sure what to do, she headed for the barn and stuck her head inside.

"Hello?" she called. "Anybody home? Ms. Morgan?"

"Hi," said a pleasant voice behind her. Val turned and saw a woman who might have been somewhere in her late thirties standing in the sunny stable yard. She was wearing riding breeches and tall, glossy boots, and her sun-streaked brown hair was pulled away from her tanned face into a thick braid that hung down her back.

"I'm Paula Morgan," the woman said, striding over to Val and shaking her hand. "And you must be Valentine Taylor, right? You're a little early. Have you been waiting long?"

"No, I just got here," Val said with a smile. She liked the look of Paula Morgan and her firm handshake. "If I'm too early, I can just hang out until you're ready for my lesson," she added.

"I'm ready any time you are," the woman replied. "I was just giving my son a few pointers. Perhaps you saw him in the ring."

"Yes, I did. He's pretty good, isn't he?"

"And getting better every day. In another year, Brad will be ready to enter his mare, Ginger, in junior jumping competition," Ms. Morgan said.

"Not for another year?" Val was surprised. "He looks good enough to ride in a show right now."

Ms. Morgan shook her head. "Oh, no. Not yet.

He only started jumping last fall. It takes time to become competent enough to show a jumper."

Val felt a little twinge of dismay. "You mean your son has been learning to jump for almost a *year* and he's not ready yet?"

Ms. Morgan smiled. "That's right. You want to learn, too, don't you, Valentine? That's what you told me when we spoke on the phone."

"Yes, I do. And please call me Val," Val said.

"Okay, Val. And I'm Paula. Tell me something about yourself. How long have you been riding?"

"Oh, for ages! My best friend and I used to ride at a stable near Essex until it closed down. But now I have my own horse," Val said eagerly. "He's a jumper, and I want to be able to ride him in a show. Can you teach me to do that?"

Paula went into the barn and Val followed her. "I'm sure I can. But first I need to get some idea of how well you ride. This is Polkadot," she said, stopping by the stall of a friendly-looking pinto. "He's all saddled up, waiting for you. Suppose we take him into the beginners' ring and you show me what you can do."

She led the pinto out to the stable yard and Val quickly mounted. Paula opened the gate into a second ring near the barn. As Val rode Polkadot into the ring, Paula climbed onto the fence and called, "Okay, walk him around once, just to get the feel of him. Then I'll tell you what to do next."

After Val and Polkadot had completed their circuit of the ring, Paula commanded, "Trot!"

They trotted.

"Canter!"

They cantered.

"Walk!"

Val had difficulty bringing the pinto from a canter to a walk, but she finally managed it. Guiding the horse over to where Paula sat, she said, "Well? Can I start learning to jump now?"

Paula stroked Polkadot's neck. She was silent so long that Val began to feel nervous. At last she said, "Val, you've never had any lessons, right?"

Val nodded.

"That's what I thought. I hope you're not going to be unhappy when I tell you that what I think you need right now is training in basic horsemanship." Seeing the crestfallen expression on Val's face, she went on, "You have natural ability, and that's good. Very, very good. But before you can start learning to jump, you have to master riding technique. Now, we'll begin at the beginning, with the way you hold your reins."

In the next forty-five minutes, Val discovered how much she didn't know. After Paula showed her how to hold the reins correctly, she taught Val how to position her feet in the stirrups, how to grip with her legs, and how to sit properly in the saddle. Then she directed her through a series of exercises designed to make her feel comfortable with everything she had practiced. By the time the lesson was over,

Val realized that there was a lot more to riding well than she had ever imagined. And she also realized that Paula was a very good teacher.

"Do you think I can become a good enough rider to enter my horse in the Horseman's Association show?" she asked Paula hopefully after she had cooled Polkadot down, unsaddled him, and returned him to his stall.

"Absolutely," Paula said without hesitation. "You're one of the best pupils I've ever had. You could certainly enter him in an equitation class on the flat. But you won't be ready for the jumping competition. As I told you before, it takes a lot of time and effort to become really good at that."

Val's shoulders slumped. "I don't want to enter The Ghost in just any old class. It wouldn't be the same thing."

"Tell me about your horse," Paula said, sitting down on a wooden bench by the stable door. "You care about him a lot, don't you?"

Val sat down next to her. "Yes, I do. He's very special."

"Funny — there was a champion jumper a few years ago called The Gray Ghost. He was owned by Longmeadow Farms in Essex. Isn't that a coincidence?"

"It's not a concidence," Val exclaimed. "It's the same horse! That's why it's so important to me to enter him in the jumping class."

Paula stared at her. "But The Gray Ghost was

retired because he developed cataracts in both eyes. Are you *sure* it's the same horse?"

"Am I ever!" Val told Paula all about buying her horse from Cassandra Merrill and the operation she hoped would save his sight. "I want him to be happy, the way he used to be. And if he can never jump again, he *won't* be happy, and neither will I," she finished.

Paula nodded. "I see." She was silent for a moment. Then she said, "Val did you ever think that there might be something else that's making him sad?"

Val shook her head. "I can't imagine what it could be. Except for his eyes, there's nothing wrong with him. He's not sick or anything — my dad's a vet, and he says he's fine. And I take real good care of him so he knows he's loved."

"What about a stablemate? Is there another animal that shares his stall?"

"No," Val said. "The Ghost lives in the barn at Animal Inn — that's my father's veterinary clinic. I work there three days a week after school and on Saturdays. If we have any large animal patients, they stay in the barn, too, but most of the time The Ghost is by himself."

"I see," Paula said again. "You know, horses are very sociable animals. In the wild, they run in herds with lots of other horses. And when The Ghost was at Longmeadow, there were other horses to keep him company. Maybe he isn't really pining because he can't jump. Maybe he's just lonely."

The idea had never occurred to Val before. Now that Paula had mentioned it, she realized that it was possible. Jocko, Andy, and Cleveland had each other, and whether Cleveland liked it or not, they'd soon have Charlie, too. There were many animals in the boarding kennel at Animal Inn. Even the patients in the infirmary weren't completely alone. Only The Ghost was on his own day in, day out, except for the time Val, Toby, or Mike spent with him.

"I remember reading a story about a racehorse that wouldn't run unless his special friend, a goat I think it was, went to the track and stayed in his stall," Val said. "Gee, Paula, you may be right. I wonder how Dad would feel about buying a goat. . . ."

Paula smiled. "Well, if you bring the subject up, please don't tell him it was my idea, or he won't let you come out here for lessons anymore. If you want to, that is, and I hope you do. You made excellent progress this afternoon."

"Thanks," Val said. "You sure taught me a lot. But I guess the biggest lesson I learned was how much more I need to learn! Could I have another lesson next Sunday, same time?"

"No problem." Paula glanced at her watch and stood up. "My next pupil is due in a few minutes so I have to saddle a horse for him. It's been a pleasure meeting you, Val." Val stood, too, and she and Paula shook hands. "See you next week. I'll be very interested to find out what you decide about The Ghost's operation.''

"So will I!'' Val said with a wry grin. "Oh, wait! I almost forgot!'' She dug into her jeans pocket and pulled out her money. As she handed the bills to Paula, she said, "That's thirty-five dollars because even though it wasn't a jumping lesson, you spent a lot of time with me.''

Kindly but firmly, Paula gave her back a ten. "Keep this and put it toward next week's session,'' she said. Before Val could protest, she waved and went into the barn.

On her way back to Essex, Val's thoughts were churning. Just a short while ago she'd been so sure that she wanted The Ghost to have surgery. But that had been before she discovered that she wouldn't be able to learn everything she needed to know in order to ride him in the jumping competition. When Lila heard that Val wasn't entering him in the horse show after all, she'd be even more obnoxious than usual!

That's what you get for bragging, she told herself as she biked down Accomac Road. And for putting the cart before the horse, like Dad said today, not to mention counting your chickens before they're hatched!

But Paula had said that by the Fourth of July she would be ready to ride The Ghost in an equitation class on the flat. Val didn't know much about showing horses, but she figured "on the flat" meant that your horse didn't jump. Even without the operation, The Ghost could see well enough for that. If she worked very hard, maybe he could win a blue ribbon after all. And what if Paula was right about his being lonely? If all he needed to make him happy was an animal friend, maybe Val could find one for him!

Chapter 8

But when Val got home, she decided not to tell her father just yet that she had decided against the surgery. She had changed her mind so many times that she didn't trust herself not to do it again. So instead, she told everybody all about her riding lesson while the Taylors and the Sparkses had supper together that evening.

"I always wanted to take riding lessons," Catherine said a little wistfully as she helped herself to some potato salad. "When I was a kid, my best friend and I used to ride at the local stable. But neither of us ever learned the fine points of horsemanship, and now I wish I had."

"It's not too late," Val said. "I've seen you ride The Ghost, and you're not bad. Paula's a really great teacher — I bet you could learn a lot from her. I know *I* did, and I've only had one lesson!"

Catherine smiled at her. "I just might look into it — *after* the wedding. Does Paula rent horses as well as board them and give riding instruction? Because if she does, perhaps your father and I could go out there some time and ride together."

"*After* the wedding," Doc added. "Erin, pass me the fried chicken, please. All that painting Teddy and I did today has given me a tremendous appetite."

In answer to Catherine's question, Val said, "I don't think Paula hires out her horses. Her sign says 'Riding Instruction and Boarding.' But I can ask her when I have my next lesson a week from today."

"Hey, I know what!" Sparky said around the chicken leg she was munching on. "Mom, you and Doc could ride The Ghost together. It'd be like the way people ride those bicycles with two seats!"

Everybody laughed at the idea of Doc and Catherine sitting on The Ghost's back, and Sparky scowled. "Well, you *could*! He's a big, strong horse. You wouldn't break his back or anything."

"Yeah, but they'd look pretty silly," Teddy said. "Two people oughta have two horses. Vallie, stop hogging all the coleslaw. I haven't had any yet."

"Catherine, have you been to Brenda's Boutique?" Erin put in. "Vallie told me that Jill said they have a dress that would be perfect for you to wear for the wedding."

"I went there yesterday," Catherine told her, "and I know the one you mean. I tried it on, and I really like it a lot. But Brenda showed me another one. . . ."

Val tuned out. Sparky had just given her an idea

for the perfect wedding present, and it was such a wonderful idea that Val couldn't think about anything else. She'd buy a tandem bicycle for her father and Catherine! Neither of them had bikes, and Doc had often talked about getting one because though he worked very hard, he didn't get nearly enough exercise. Yes, a bicycle built for two was the solution to Val's problem. It met all her requirements — it was something they didn't already have, it was useful, and it was something they could share.

Val decided that right after school tomorrow, she'd check out the stores in town. She was sure that Schaeffer's Sporting Goods would have a tandem bicycle. And if they didn't, there was always Handy Hardware, and the big Montgomery Ward at the mall. Humming under her breath, Val piled some pasta salad on her plate.

"What's that song, Vallie?" Teddy asked.

His question took her by surprise. The tune had just popped into her head, and she hadn't really thought about it at all. Now that she did, she grinned and sang loud, " 'We won't have a stylish marriage, I can't afford a carriage. But you'll look sweet upon the seat of a bicycle built for two'!"

Doc laughed. "Well, now, from what Catherine and Erin have been saying about what all you ladies will be wearing, it's going to be a *very* stylish marriage."

"Oh, Vallie, that reminds me," Erin said

quickly. "I've decided not to wear my toe shoes, so you and Sparky and I have to shop for *real* shoes because they have to be — "

"Dyed to match our dresses. I know," Val finished for her. "Jill already told me."

"Can we meet tomorrow after school?" Sparky asked eagerly. "Erin and me could meet you at Francie's Footwear, couldn't we, Erin?"

"Francie's Footwear!" Teddy groaned. "Gimme a break!" He glared at his stepsister-to-be. "You *can't* go shopping for dopey shoes tomorrow 'cause we're supposed to be playing softball with the gang tomorrow afternoon, and you're the catcher!"

"I have something else important to do, too," Val said, thinking of her plan to search for a tandem bike.

"It can't be as important as getting the right shoes for the wedding," Erin told her. "You have awfully big feet, you know, Vallie. What if the store has to order them specially for you? It could take *ages*!" Turning to Teddy, she added, "Why can't Billy or Eric catch your balls? It doesn't sound very complicated."

"That's because you don't know anything about softball," Teddy grumbled. "All you know about is ballet dancing and dumb stuff like that!"

"Ballet dancing is *not* dumb!" Erin yelled. "What's *really* dumb is playing stupid games where people throw balls at each other and try to hit them far way so they can run around in a circle and end up where they started from!"

"*Children!*" Doc and Catherine said at the same time.

"Let's not argue, okay?" Catherine smiled at Teddy and Erin. "I'm sure we can work out something that won't ruin everybody's plans. If the girls order their shoes right after school, maybe the game could start a little late and Philomena could still catch for your team, Teddy. And Val could do whatever she has to do then, too, right, Val?"

"Sure," Val agreed. "Sounds good to me." How long could it take to buy three pairs of shoes? She'd have plenty of time to find her extra-special present afterward. She glanced down at the well-worn leather boots she hadn't taken off since her riding lesson, wishing that bridesmaids could wear something really comfortable on their feet. Val loved to go barefoot, and she decided then and there that if she ever got married, neither she nor her bridesmaids would wear any shoes at all!

Monday's shopping expedition took longer than anyone thought it would. Francie's Footwear didn't have dyeable shoes in the girls' sizes. And by the time Val, Erin, and Sparky had found a store that could fit all three of them and match the fabric sample Erin had brought along, it was too late for Sparky's softball game or for Val to check out places that might sell tandem bikes. That meant she wouldn't be able to start her search until Thursday, since she would be working the next two days at Animal Inn.

But that would be all right, Val told herself as she biked out to the clinic after school on Tuesday. Though there were less than three weeks until the wedding, she would still have plenty of time to find what she was looking for, or even to order it if none of the stores had one in stock.

As Val slowed to a stop in the parking lot of Animal Inn, she noticed a small horse trailer attached to a pickup truck in front of the Large Animal Clinic. Remembering what Paula had said about horses needing companionship, Val hoped that the patient wasn't too sick to be a friend for The Ghost. But she doubted it, because people didn't usually bring large animals to the clinic unless they were too ill for Doc to treat them at the farm.

She hurried into the Small Animal Clinic, and as soon as Pat saw her, she said, "Oh, Vallie, go see your dad! He has something to tell you!" Pat sounded excited, but the expression on her round face was solemn, as though she were both happy and sad.

Puzzled, Val said, "Okay. Where is he?"

"He's in his office with Junior Miller," Pat told her. She sighed. "Poor Junior! The funeral was yesterday, you know. I read the notice in the *Gazette*."

Val stared at her. "What funeral? Did old Mr. Miller die?"

Pat nodded sorrowfully. "Real sudden, too. He

just passed away in his sleep. That's why Junior's here. He brought Dancer because . . ." She pursed her lips. "Well, I mustn't tell you anything else. You go talk to Doc. He'll give you all the details."

Val felt very sorry for Junior — and for Mr. Miller. She hadn't known Junior's father very well because he had been sick for so long, but she knew how fond he had been of his chestnut mare. If Dancer was sick, too, that made it even worse. It must have been Dancer who had arrived in the trailer she'd seen. But Dancer had looked perfectly fine only a week ago.

Opening the door behind the receptionist's desk, Val went down the hall to her father's private office. As she approached, she heard Junior saying, ". . . so that's how it is, Doc. I'm gonna sell the farm, lock, stock, and barrel, and move to York. My buddy's got an auto repair shop there, and he wants me to go in with him. He says we can make good money fixin' cars, and that sounds fine to me. I always liked cars better'n animals anyway. Now that Pop's gone, there's no sense me stayin' on the farm. Never liked farmin' at all, to tell you the truth. And now . . ."

Val knocked softly on the open door. "Uh — hi, Dad. Pat said you wanted to see me?"

Doc smiled at her. "Come on in, honey."

"Hi, Vallie," Junior said. "Guess you heard about Pop, huh?"

"Pat just told me," Val replied. "I'm awfully sorry, Junior." She felt awkward and uncomfortable, wondering if there was something else she ought to say, but she couldn't think of anything.

"He passed away real peaceful," Junior said. "Last Friday, it was. Real nice funeral, too — Pop would've been pleased to see how many people showed up."

"That's good," Val mumbled. Eager to change the subject, she added, "Pat said you brought Dancer in. Is she sick, or did she get hurt?"

Junior shook his head. "Nope. She's just fine."

Val was confused. "If there's nothing wrong with her, what's she doing at Animal Inn?"

Doc and Junior looked at each other. "You want to tell her?" Junior asked.

"I think I'll leave it up to you," Doc said, "since you're carrying out your father's wish."

More confused that ever, Val said, "Tell me what? What are you talking about?"

"Well now, Vallie, it's like this," Junior began, hitching up his faded overalls. "Before Pop passed on, he made a will leavin' everything to me — or *almost* everything, anyways."

Val waited for him to continue, wondering what old Mr. Miller's will had to do with her. After a long pause, Junior went on, "But he left something to you, too."

"He did?" Val's eyes widened.

Junior nodded. "Yep, he did. Want to try to guess what it is?"

"I couldn't possibly!" Val exclaimed. "I think you'd better tell me."

"All right, then, I will." Junior smiled at her. "It's Dancer."

Val could hardly believe her ears. "Dancer?" she gasped. "He left Dancer to *me*? But why? I mean, that's wonderful, but . . . but . . ."

"Like I told you the other day when you and Doc was out at the farm, Pop knew how much you care about animals," Junior said, his smile broadening. "And likewise, he knew that I don't. Guess he wanted to make sure I didn't sell that mare to just anybody, so he left her to you. It's all down in black and white — 'To Valentine Taylor, my mare Dancer, her bridle and saddle, and the horse blanket I bought two years ago that's still like new.' That's what his will says, Vallie, so Dancer's all yours. The way I figure it, you might as well keep the horse trailer, too. I'm sure not gonna need it down in York at the garage!"

"I — I don't know what to say," Val mumbled. She looked at her father. "Dad, is it all right?" There was a rule in the Taylor family concerning pets: Nobody could get a new one unless everybody in the family agreed. But a horse wasn't exactly a pet, and there was nothing in the rule about animals that were left to you in somebody's will!

"Yes, Vallie, it's all right," Doc said. "And as for what to say, how about, thank you?"

"Oh, thank you, Junior!" Val cried. "The Ghost needs a friend, and I didn't know how to go about getting him one. But now he won't be lonely anymore!" She stood on tiptoe and kissed Junior's stubbly cheek.

Junior's face turned bright red. "Well now, no need to thank me," he said. "It was Pop's doing, not mine. Guess I better unhitch the trailer from my truck, and then I'll be going. See ya, Doc." He started out the door, then turned and added, "Dancer's still in the trailer, by the way. Guess you better take her out."

"I can do that," Toby said eagerly. Val hadn't seen him standing in the hall, but she realized now that he must have heard most of what they had been saying.

Completely forgetting that she was mad at Toby, she gave him a big grin. "We'll do it together! Come on, Toby. We can put Dancer in the empty stall next to The Ghost's. Boy, will he be surprised when I bring him in from the pasture!"

A few minutes later, Junior drove away in his pickup truck, and Val and Toby brought the mare into the barn. Val held onto Dancer's halter while Toby spread clean, sweet-smelling straw on the floor of the stall that would be hers.

"She looks kinda mangy," Toby said. "She's all furry, like a dog or something."

"That's because nobody has taken proper care

of her," Val told him. "All that fuzz is her winter coat. After I give her a good currying and brush her a lot, she'll be sleek and shiny just like The Ghost."

The mare tossed her head and danced around a little, living up to her name.

"So what are you going to do with her?" Toby asked. "You can't ride two horses at the same time. It's like what you were saying about wedding presents for Catherine and Doc. They've got two of everything, and they only need one."

"Yeah, I know. But horses aren't the same thing as toasters or blenders. They need companionship. That's what Paula said."

"Who's Paula?"

As Val led Dancer into her stall, she realized that she hadn't told Toby about the riding lessons. She hadn't told him anything at all lately, and she'd missed sharing her experiences with the boy who was her second-best friend next to Jill. So she explained who Paula was, and when she had finished, Toby agreed that her riding teacher sounded pretty neat.

"Does that mean you're not going to enter The Ghost in the jumping competition at the horse show?" he asked. "And you're not going to make him have that operation?"

"I'm not sure," Val admitted. "The horse show's not until July, and it's only April. But I've been thinking that maybe I'll enter an equitation class instead."

Toby frowned. "What's that?"

"Equitation means horsemanship. Pauls says I'll be ready for that if I keep on taking lessons, but it'll take much longer for me to learn to jump. I didn't realize how hard you had to work to become a really good jumper."

Avoiding Toby's eyes, Val concentrated on removing a burr from Dancer's mane. "I guess maybe you were right about me being a show-off," she murmured. "I *did* want to show off for Lila and the Merrills, and I thought it would be easy once The Ghost could see again. But that was before I knew how much depended on the rider in a jumping class. I'm just not good enough yet. Maybe I never will be."

"Oh, I bet you will some day," Toby said with a friendly grin. "You're pretty stubborn, and when you set your mind to something, you hang in there until you do it."

Val grinned, too. "Thanks — I think!" She glanced at her watch. "Oh, wow! It's almost four o'clock and all we've done so far is get Dancer settled in her new home. We'd better get back to the clinic." Patting the mare's soft nose, she added, "Sorry, girl, but I'll have to groom you later, after office hours. And then I'll introduce you to The Ghost. I just know the two of you are going to be good friends!"

Chapter
9

As soon as the last patient had been treated, Doc took off on a house call, telling Val he'd see her at supper. Usually Val would have gone along with him, but not today. She was too eager to get back to her new horse and to see The Ghost's reaction when he discovered Dancer in the stall next to his.

Pausing only to grab the apple Doc hadn't eaten for lunch from the clinic's small refrigerator, Val raced to the barn. The chestnut mare stuck her head out over the door of her stall and whickered a welcome. And when Val held out the bright red apple on the palm of her hand, Dancer gobbled it up as though she hadn't had a treat in months.

"And I bet you haven't, either," Val said, stroking the mare's neck. "Nobody paid much attention to you at all after old Mr. Miller got sick, did they? Well, everything's going to be different now. And *you're* going to be different, too — at least you're going to *look* different, because the first thing I'm going to do is groom you until you're as beautiful as The Ghost!"

She hurried to the empty stall she and Toby had fixed up as a tack room when Val had first bought the dapple-gray gelding. Now Dancer's saddle and bridle hung next to The Ghost's, and the almost-new horse blanket was neatly folded on top of the small chest of drawers where the curry combs and brushes were stored. Val took one of each back to Dancer's stall and got to work. She used the curry comb first, to remove the dried mud and loose hair from the mare's coat. Soon the air was so filled with dust that Val began to cough and sneeze. But Dancer made it clear by the way she just stood there with half-closed eyes that she was as happy as a horse could be.

"Feels good, doesn't it?" Val asked, smiling — and sneezing. "If the weather were a little warmer and it wasn't so late, I'd take you outside and give you a shower with the hose. But that'll have to wait for a week or so."

Dancer stamped and snorted, as though to say that was fine with her, and Val traded the curry comb for the brush. She brushed the mare's forelock, mane, and tail, and then gave her a thorough going-over from nose to rump, removing still more dust and fuzz. At the end of half an hour, Dancer looked like a different horse. Her reddish-brown coat wasn't as satiny as The Ghost's, but she no longer looked as though she was covered with scruffy fur.

Pleased with the result of her efforts, Val gave Dancer a pat and said, "Okay, girl, that's it for now. I'll be right back — I'm going to bring The Ghost in from the pasture!"

As she slipped out of Dancer's stall and headed for the barn door, Val could hardly believe that Dancer was really hers. Just to make sure that she wasn't making the whole thing up, she sneaked a peek over her shoulder. Sure enough, there was Dancer right where Val had left her, in the stall next to The Ghost's, munching contentedly on a mouthful of fresh, sweet hay.

"Imagine Junior liking cars better than horses," Val said to herself, hurrying to the pasture. She couldn't wait to introduce The Ghost to his new companion.

A moment later, the dapple-gray gelding ambled over to the fence in response to Val's low whistle. She opened the gate and ran to him, throwing her arms around his neck. "Oh, Ghost, do I have a surprise for you!" she cried. Then she took hold of his halter and led him toward the barn. He plodded after her without much interest, swishing his silvery tail. With mounting excitement, Val guided him through the barn door.

At the sound of The Ghost's hooves, Dancer poked her head out. The minute she saw the other horse, she whinnied. The Ghost's ears perked up. He raised his head and quickened his step.

"That's the surprise," Val told him, grinning

from ear to ear. "Meet your new neighbor! Her name's Dancer, and she's not sick or anything. She's not a patient — she's going to live here from now on, just like you!"

She led The Ghost right over to Dancer's stall, and held her breath as the two horses gazed at each other. Slowly, very slowly, The Ghost stretched out his satiny neck until his nose was within inches of Dancer's. The mare's nostrils flared. Then she laid back her ears and nipped at The Ghost with her strong, yellow teeth. Taken by surprise, The Ghost let out a startled snort and backed away.

"Dancer!" Val cried. "You stop that this minute!"

Now The Ghost lunged forward, ears flattened, and tried to nip at Dancer.

"Ghost! Cut it out! Is that any way to behave?" Val was very distressed. "What's the matter with you two? You're supposed to be friends!"

"How can they be friends if they ain't had time to find out if they like each other or not?" Mike Strickler asked.

Val hadn't seen Mike come into the barn, but there he was, leaning on his push broom and peering at her from beneath the visor of his battered cap that had the words DRUCKER'S FEED STORE printed on the crown. The wiry little old man always reminded Val of a Pennsylvania Dutch leprechaun, even though she knew there was no such thing.

"But they're both horses," Val said, struggling

to control The Ghost, who was trying to pull away from her grip on his halter. "And they've both been alone for a long time! They ought to be happy to be together!"

Mike shrugged. "Maybe they oughta be, but they ain't," he said calmly. "Give 'em a chance, Vallie. Horses is just like people. They gotta get to know each other before they decide if they're gonna be pals. How'd you like it if somebody marched you up to a stranger and told you to be friends right away?"

"I guess I wouldn't be too thrilled about it," Val admitted. The Ghost had calmed down a little, and she stroked him gently. "But I sure wouldn't try to take a bite out of the other person!"

Grinning, Mike said, "Mebbe not, but then you ain't a horse." He propped his broom against one of the stall doors. "Give 'em time, Vallie."

Val sighed. "I guess you're right. I was just so excited about The Ghost having Dancer to keep him company that it never occurred to me they might not be happy about it, too. Maybe after they've been next-door neighbors for a while, they'll learn to like each other."

She led The Ghost into his stall, but as soon as she did, Dancer kicked the wall between them, and The Ghost kicked back.

"Oh, no," Val wailed. "Do you think they'll keep this up all night?"

"Could be," Mike said cheerfully. " 'Course, I'll

be here to keep an eye on 'em, but if I was you, I'd move that mare to one of them empty stalls across the way. Put 'er in the big loose box right opposite The Ghost. Remember, she's been runnin' free in Millers' pasture for a long time. She's not used to bein' cooped up like this, let alone havin' another horse to deal with. That way the two of 'em can kinda check each other out from a distance. Then when they know each other a little better, you can move her back.''

Val brightened. "That's a good idea, Mike. Is there lots of clean straw in the loose box?''

"Sure there is,'' Mike said. "I keep all them stalls clean as a whistle, Vallie, you know that. Want me to take Dancer over there now while you stay with The Ghost?''

Val nodded, and she and The Ghost watched Mike lead the mare across the aisle that separated the two rows of stalls. "You sure spruced her up real good,'' Mike said approvingly. "She didn't look like much before, and that's the truth.'' He opened the door to the loose box and gave Dancer a slap on the rump as she trotted inside. Latching the door behind her, he went on, "Pat told me about Roy Miller leavin' you his horse, so I came right over here to have a look.'' He grinned at Val. "You gonna stay here with her all night?''

Val looked at her watch. "Omigosh, it's almost six! Dad's probably home already, and everybody will be wondering where I am.'' She gave The Ghost a quick hug, then hurried out of his stall. "See you tomorrow, Dancer. Mike, you'll visit them every now and then tonight, won't you, just to make sure everything's okay?"

"I told you I would," Mike said. "And while I'm at it, I'll explain to both of 'em how they're supposed to behave. Don't you worry none, Vallie. They're gonna get along just fine."

Glancing from The Ghost to Dancer, who were eyeing each other cautiously across the broad aisle, Val crossed her fingers. "I sure hope you're right, because if you're not, I've got a real problem on my hands!"

When Val got home, she found her family just sitting down to supper at the kitchen table. Doc had told Teddy and Erin about Dancer, and they were both bursting with questions that Val answered while she ate.

"Boy, is that ever cool!" Teddy said when Val had finished telling them all the details. "My sister has *two* horses! Wait till I tell Sparky and the rest of the gang! Will you let us ride Dancer sometimes, Vallie?"

"Sure," Val replied, "but not right away. She hasn't been ridden hardly at all lately, so she'll probably be pretty frisky for a while. You'll have to wait until she gets used to having someone on her back again."

"I wish I could ride her, too," Erin said, helping

herself to some salad. "But Miss Tamara says that horseback riding isn't good for ballet dancers. It stretches their muscles the wrong way. I want to see Dancer, though. Let's see — I have ballet class after school tomorrow, so I can't go to Animal Inn then, and I can't come Thursday, either, because you and Sparky and I have some more shopping to do for the wedding. . . ."

In her excitement about Dancer, Val had actually forgotten all about the wedding. Now that Erin had reminded her, she remembered that Thursday was when she planned to look for the tandem bicycle for Catherine and Doc. "Sorry, Erin," she said. "I have something else to do on Thursday after school."

"What could there possibly be left to buy?" Doc asked. "Mrs. Racer is making your dresses, and you've all ordered your shoes."

"I bet I know!" Teddy shouted. "*Underwear!* I bet you need extra-special fancy wedding underwear!"

"As a matter of fact, we do," Erin said, much to Val's amazement.

"You're kidding, right?" she asked her sister.

"Well, it's not exactly underwear," Erin replied. "But it's somethihg to wear under our dresses. Crinolines!"

"Crinolines?" Teddy choked. "Sounds like a disease!" He crossed his eyes, clutched at his throat, and toppled off his chair, moaning, "Aaargh! I've got *crinolines*! Somebody call the doctor!" The dogs immediately dashed in from the dining room where they had been lying and jumped on him, licking his face and wagging their tails.

"Jocko and Andy, *out!*" Doc said sternly. "Teddy, *up*. Doctor's orders!"

Grinning, Teddy got back onto his chair and the dogs obediently trotted back into the dining room. "Well, it *does* sound like a disease," Teddy insisted.

"For your information, crinolines are stiff, ruffly petticoats that you wear to make the skirt of your dress stick out," Erin said with a sniff.

"Oh, no I don't!" Teddy giggled. "Maybe *you* do, but not me!"

Doc put a hand on Teddy's forehead. Looking very solemn, he said, "Just as I suspected. Slightly feverish. Young man, I'm afraid you have a severe case of the sillies! And you know what the cure for that is?"

Still laughing, Teddy shook his head.

"Clearing the table," Doc told him, and Teddy groaned. But he started removing the dirty dishes and putting them in the sink.

"*Anyway,*" Erin went on, "we have to buy crinolines or our skirts will look all droopy, and they'll probably be harder to find than the shoes were. Olivia said her mother was looking for one, and she had to go all the way to Harrisburg before she found what she wanted. That's why we have to start looking on Thursday."

"Okay," Val sighed. "But I really do have something very important to take care of, so let's look real fast."

"Speaking of clothes for the wedding," Doc said as he went over to the refrigerator and took out the bowl of chocolate pudding Mrs. Racer had made for dessert, "Teddy and I are going to have to do some serious shopping, too. I don't have a decent lightweight suit, and Teddy doesn't have a suit at all, decent or otherwise."

"Gimme a break," Teddy exclaimed. "A *suit*? I've gotta wear a *suit*? I *hate* suits!"

Doc grinned. "You know something, Teddy? So do I. But for this one very special occasion, we'll have to grin and bear it. Or perhaps I should say, grin and *wear* it!"

Later that evening, after Val had fed her rabbits, the chickens, and the duck, she was on her way up to her new third-floor bedroom when Doc called her into his study.

"I've been wondering if you've come to a decision about The Ghost's surgery," he said as Val sat on the hassock in front of his big leather armchair. "I really should call Dr. Weintraub by the end of this week to let him know one way or the other."

Val said, "I know, Dad. I'm sorry it's taken me so long, but I keep changing my mind! On the way out to Paula's on Sunday, I was positive I wanted to go ahead with it, but after I talked to her, I was almost as positive that I didn't. Paula said that maybe The

Ghost was sad because he was lonely, not because he couldn't jump. And so when Junior Miller gave Dancer to me today, I hoped The Ghost would cheer up as soon as he met her. But he didn't, and she doesn't like him, either!"

She hadn't said anything about the horses' reactions to each other before, but now Val told Doc what had happened. She finished by saying, "Mike thinks they just need time, and then they'll be friends. But what if he's wrong?"

Doc smiled at her. "Honey, Mike Strickler knows more about animals than just about anybody I've ever met. I'd be inclined to take his word for it. Wait and see. Be patient. I know it's hard, but try, okay?"

"Okay," Val said. Then she added, "I've just about decided to enter The Ghost in an equitation class instead of a jumping class. Paula says I'll be ready for that by July, but it'll take much longer for me to learn to jump. Who knows — maybe we can win a blue ribbon anyway. That would prove The Ghost's still a champion, wouldn't it?"

"It would indeed," her father agreed. "And even if he doesn't win a blue, he'll always be a champion, you know. He's already proved that. Does this mean that you've decided against the operation?"

After a long pause, Val nodded. "I guess it does. But you'd better call Dr. Weintraub real soon, or else I'll probably change my mind again!"

* * *

Now that the question of The Ghost's surgery had finally been settled, Val felt as if a great load had been lifted from her mind. And she felt even better about her decision as day followed day and the relationship between the dapple-gray gelding and the chestnut mare improved. Mike swore it was because he gave them both a good talking-to every night. But whatever the reason, Val was delighted. If The Ghost had been lonely and bored before, he certainly wasn't anymore. The youthful spring was back in his step, and he held his handsome head high, looking every bit the champion he was.

As for Dancer, she looked prettier and shinier every day, thanks to Val's and Toby's careful grooming and the quantities of oats, corn, and sweet hay they fed her. Val had wondered if she would be able to handle the mare because Dancer hadn't been ridden in so long. But she discovered that once Dancer found out that Val knew what she was doing, she was as gentle as a lamb. Val realized that she had Paula to thank for that, and Val told her so at her next riding lesson.

Paula was amazed by the story of Val's unexpected legacy, and glad to hear that The Ghost was acting like his old self again.

"I'm sure that being together is the best thing in the world for both of them," she told Val. "Just be patient, and you'll see that they'll end up being the best of friends."

Val grinned. "That's what my father said. I'm not all that good at being patient, but I'm giving it my best shot."

It wasn't until Val's lesson was over and she was about to leave that she remembered promising Catherine to ask if Paula rented any of her horses to riders. In answer to her question, Paula said she didn't. But now that Val had two horses of her own, it didn't matter very much. Catherine and Doc would be able to ride Dancer and The Ghost whenever they wanted, though Val knew they wouldn't have time until after the wedding.

But the wedding date was coming closer and closer, and Val still had one major problem to solve. There wasn't a single store in Essex that had a tandem bike in stock, she discovered to her dismay. Some of the people she talked to didn't even know what a tandem bicycle was!

"I bet Mom would drive us to York, or even Harrisburg to look for one," Jill said when Val told her about it later the following week. "But even if we found one, I don't see how we could fit it in our little car. You're right, Val — a bicycle built for two is a terrific idea, but maybe you'd better start trying to think of something else."

"I *have* been trying," Val sighed, "but I haven't come up with anything at all."

"There's always that vase we saw in Reineman's a couple of weeks ago," Jill reminded her. "It's probably awfully expensive, but now that you're not paying for The Ghost's operation, you can certainly afford it."

"Yeah, I know. but it's just so — so *usual*," Val said. "I want something *un*usual. And I'm not going to give up until I find out what it is!"

On Saturday at Animal Inn, she asked Toby if he had any suggestions. They were letting the dogs in the boarding kennel out into the run for their daily exercise. "Search me," Toby said as he opened the door of one the cages. "I only just figured out what I'm going to give them myself."

"What is it?" Val asked, guiding the Airedale that leaped out of the cage in the direction of the run. "Maybe it will give me some ideas."

"Well, I talked it over with Mom and Dad, and we decided I oughta give them a gift certificate to our ice cream parlor in town. Free ice cream any time they want for a whole year!" Toby looked very pleased, and Val was impressed.

"That's a fabulous present!" Val cried. "I didn't know Curran's Ice Cream Parlor had gift certificates."

"We don't," Toby told her. "My mom made a special one just for Catherine and Doc. She does calligraphy, and it looks really neat. Do you think they'll like it?"

"Oh, yes," Val said. "And so will the rest of us!" she added with a grin.

"Hey, wait a minute! The gift certificate's only

good for Doc and Catherine, not the whole family!" Toby said.

Laughing, Val said, "I was just kidding. But it really is a great idea, Toby." Suddenly she had an idea of her own. "Toby! Listen to this! What if I asked Paula Morgan for a gift certificate for riding lessons for them? Maybe five lessons each during the summer. Catherine was saying just the other day that she wished she'd taken lessons when she was a kid, and I bet Dad would like that, too. He used to ride a lot, but he's pretty rusty now. And then they could really enjoy riding The Ghost and Dancer." That gave her still another idea, but she decided not to mention it to Toby yet. It would be a surprise for everyone, not just her father and Catherine! Val was so happy that she started dancing around the room. "Oh, Toby, thanks! You've just solved my problem. I'm going to call Paula right now!"

Paula was happy to provide Val with a gift certificate for Doc's and Catherine's riding lessons. She promised to put a letter in the mail that very day so Val would get it in time for the wedding. Val agreed to pay the full amount next Sunday when she had her own lesson.

That evening after Animal Inn closed, Val waited for Mike Strickler to come into the barn. As soon as he did, she told him about the second part of her plan because he was a very important part of it.

"Why, sure, Vallie, I can do that," Mike said,

grinning from ear to ear. "No problem at all. I'll take care of it on my way to your house for the wedding. You're gonna call Miss Maggie to let her know what's happenin', right?"

"I'll call her as soon as I get home," Val told him. "And please don't say anything about this to anybody else, Mike. I want it to stay a secret until the reception!"

Chapter 10

And then all of a sudden the great day arrived. The morning flew by in total confusion as last-minute preparations were completed. Val had gone to Animal Inn with Doc to check on the patients in the infirmary, and Doc had given careful instructions to Pat's son-in-law, whom he had hired to take care of the animals while the clinic was closed for the day. Now, at half-past one in the afternoon, everybody but Val was busy changing into their wedding finery for the ceremony that was scheduled for two o'clock.

Val was still in her shorts and T-shirt because she had been helping Mrs. Racer and Mrs. Wilson finish arranging the flowers in the living room. Then she had let the dogs out into the backyard, and spent what seemed like ages searching for Cleveland. She found her cat at last, hiding under the living room sofa to escape from all the hustle and bustle. Val dragged him out and carried him upstairs, intending to shut him in her third-floor bedroom until after the wedding. She was hurrying through the second-floor hall when Erin burst out of her bedroom.

"Panty hose!" Erin wailed.

Val paused. "What about panty hose?" she asked, puzzled.

"I don't have any! I completely forgot to buy them," Erin cried.

"You could wear white socks like mine," Sparky offered, popping out of the door to Val's old bedroom that was now hers. Catherine had dropped Sparky off an hour ago so she could dress with the other bridesmaids. Then Catherine had returned to her almost empty house to get dressed herself. With her hair rolled up in pink plastic curlers all over her head, Sparky looked so funny that Val had a hard time keeping a straight face.

"No, I can't, " Erin moaned. "It would completely *ruin* the effect!"

"What about your ballet tights?" Doc suggested, sticking his head out of his room. "You have dozens of pairs of pink ones."

"Ballet tights — good idea!" Erin disappeared into her room, closing the door behind her.

"Dad!" Teddy yelled. "I can't tie this dumb tie! Help!"

"In a minute, Teddy. Just let me put on my shoes," Doc said as he went back inside.

"When are you gonna get dressed, Val?" Sparky asked. "It's getting awful late."

"I know," Val said, clutching her struggling cat. "I'm going to do it right now."

As she started up the steps, Sparky called after her, "Erin's gonna help me get dressed. And she's gonna fix my hair, too. Wait till you see my curls!"

"Curls! Yuck!" Teddy shouted. "Dad, hurry up! I'm strangling myself!"

Giggling, Val said to Cleveland, "I bet you're glad you're a cat so you don't have to bother with any of this stuff."

"*Rraaoow*," Cleveland agreed.

Less than twenty minutes later, showered, shampooed, and fully dressed, Val raced down the stairs and headed for the kitchen where the rest of the wedding party had gathered. As she sped past the living room, she saw that most of the guests had already arrived — all but Miss Maggie, who had phoned the previous night to say that much as she would like to attend, the arrangements for the reception were going to keep her too busy, and the staff she had hired would need her supervision.

After Doc had spoken to her, Val did, too, using the phone in the upstairs hall so nobody would hear their conversation. She and Miss Maggie had some secret arrangements of their own to discuss, and when they had, Miss Maggie said, "Just leave everything to Mike and me, Valentine. It will work out perfectly, I guarantee." Knowing Miss Maggie, Val was sure it would.

Now she dashed through the kitchen doorway and skidded to a stop in her pale pink linen pumps, staring wide-eyed at her family. "Oh, you all look *beautiful*!" she said softly.

And they did, every last one of them. She had never seen her father or her little brother look so handsome, and Sparky and Erin looked like a pair of lovely dolls in their matching rose-colored dresses. Sparky's curls were a great success, and Erin's silvery-blonde hair, which she usually wore in a ballerina knot, hung loose over her shoulders — like a fairy tale princess, Val thought.

"You look beautiful, too, honey," Doc said, smiling at her.

"Yeah, Vallie, you don't look half bad," Teddy added.

Just then Mrs. Racer bustled in from the dining room, carrying four bouquets of fresh-cut flowers. Her eyes were sparkling and her cheeks flushed with excitement as she handed a bouquet to each of the girls. "The judge is here," she whispered, "and Toby's all ready to play the wedding march on the stereo."

Suddenly Val realized that someone was missing. "Where's Catherine?" she asked. "We can't start without her!"

"I'm in here," said a muffled voice from behind the closed pantry door. "And I'm ready whenever the rest of you are."

Val blinked. "What's she doing in there?" she asked in astonishment.

"Because it's bad luck for the bride and groom

to see each other before the ceremony," Mrs. Racer said briskly. "I'll let her out after Doc and Teddy go into the living room."

"Then you can let her out now," Doc said, "because here we go!"

Side by side, he and Teddy marched solemnly out the kitchen door into the dining room. Val, Erin, and Sparky watched them pass through the wide arch between the dining room and living room and stand next to Judge Gross in front of the flower-laden fireplace. Mrs. Racer opened the pantry door, and Catherine stepped out, looking so lovely in her pale lilac dress that Val caught her breath.

"Oh, Catherine!" she exclaimed. "You're the most beautiful of all!"

Sparky ran over to give her mother a hug. "You sure are, Mom!"

Erin stood on tiptoe and kissed Catherine's cheek. "You look like the Lilac Fairy in *Sleeping Beauty*," she said.

Catherine smiled at all of them. "Thank you, daughters." She took the bouquet that Mrs. Racer handed her, and as she did, the "Wedding March" from *Lohengrin* began to play.

Beaming, Mrs. Racer hurried off to take her place with her son, Henry, among the guests, and Erin gave Sparky a little shove. "You're first," she whispered. Sparky nodded and began taking tiny little steps, followed by Erin, Val, and finally, Catherine.

As Val entered the living room, she glanced around at all the dear, familiar faces. She felt a lump in her throat and sudden tears stung her eyes. Looking at Mrs. Racer, Val saw that the old lady was sniffling into a large white handkerchief. But she knew that Mrs. Racer's tears, like her own, were tears of happiness.

Now that the wedding party was all assembled, Catherine gave Val her bouquet and took Doc's hand. The music stopped, and the ruddy, white-haired judge began to read the words of the ceremony from his little black book. A new life was beginning for all of them, Val thought. And it would be a *good* life, she was absolutely sure.

"That was the nicest wedding I've ever been to," Donna Hartman told Val an hour later. "And little Valentine thought so, too, didn't you, sweetie?" she said to the plump, bonneted baby in her arms.

Val was standing with Donna and her husband, Jim, next to one of the refreshment tables on Miss Maggie's velvety lawn, surrounded by hundreds of laughing, chattering guests. Sunlight filtered down through the leaves of the trees above them, glancing off silver serving dishes piled high with luscious food and dappling the white damask tablecloth with light and shade.

Smiling at her small namesake, Val said, "She was as good as gold. I didn't hear a peep out of her the whole time."

"Too bad she's not old enough to have some of this stuff, whatever it is." Jim was digging into a plateful of assorted goodies. "This sure is some spread! Aren't you going to eat anything, Vallie? Try the shrimp — at least I know what *they* are. There must be thousands of 'em!"

"I'll eat later," Val told him. "Right now I want to find Mike. There's something real important I have to talk to him about!"

But she didn't get very far because friends and neighbors kept stopping her to offer their best wishes and congratulations on her new stepmother and step-sister. To Val's amazement, one of the well-wishers was Lila Bascombe.

"Oh, Val, isn't this just the *loveliest* party?" Lila gushed. "Don't you *adore* weddings? And Mrs. Sparks — oops," she giggled, "I mean Mrs. *Taylor* looks absolutely super in that divine lavender dress! I guess it won't be too terrible having a stepmother now that you know she has good taste."

Val smiled sweetly at her. "Gee, Lila, I always knew Catherine had good taste. She agreed to marry Dad, didn't she?"

"And your father looks awfully handsome today, not at all like he usually does. . . . Oh dear, I didn't mean that the way it sounded," Lila rattled on. "You look pretty good yourself, Val. That dress is very becoming to you even though it's handmade. The puffy sleeves make your shoulders look less broad, and the full skirt actually makes your waist look small!"

"I like your dress, too, Lila," Val said, glancing at the ruffled and beribboned creation Lila was wearing, "even though it's *not* handmade. Sorry I can't stand here and talk some more, but I'm looking for somebody. Why don't you go eat a shrimp or something?"

Lila shuddered delicately. "I couldn't *possibly*! I'm terribly allergic to shrimp — they make me swell up and turn bright red."

"Then have two or three," Val called over her shoulder, grinning broadly.

She weaved her way through the crowd, trying not to step on Miss Maggie's many dogs, who were constantly underfoot, begging for treats. She didn't see Mike Strickler anywhere, which wasn't too surprising because Mike was very short and many of the other guests were very tall. But she did see Miss Maggie not too far away, helping some of the waiters pour champagne into crystal goblets set out on dozens of silver trays. Miss Maggie was dressed in a turquoise silk sari shot through with golden threads. She wore long, dangling gold earrings, and dozens of golden bangle bracelets on each tanned arm. Val thought she looked very exotic, and much younger that her eighty-odd years.

"Afternoon, Valentine," Miss Maggie said when Val finally reached her. "It's almost time to toast the bride and groom. Are you ready to do your thing?" Her bright blue eyes sparkled with excitement.

"Oh, yes!" Val said. "But I can't find Mike. You

don't think anything's gone wrong, do you?"

"Of course not." Miss Maggie handed an empty champagne bottle to a passing waiter, who gave her a full one in exchange. "Everything worked out just the way we planned. He's over there, behind the rhododendrons, keeping an eye on . . ." she glanced around, then whispered, ". . . you know what."

"He didn't have any trouble bringing them over here?" Val asked.

"None at all. After he delivered the first one, he went back and got the other."

The waiters began picking up the trays and started circulating among the guests, offering them glasses of champagne, while others passed out cups of fruit punch.

"You'd better scoot," Miss Maggie said to Val. "Mike's waiting."

Val gave her a quick hug and a kiss on her weathered cheek. "Thanks for everything, Miss Maggie!" she said. Then she raced toward the hedge of rhododendrons, passing Jill, Toby, and several of her other friends on the way. When they called to her, she just kept on going. "Talk to you later," she shouted.

"I was beginnin' to think you'd forgotten all about us," Mike said as she ran up to him. "And they was, too. The Ghost and Dancer are gettin' mighty impatient."

Val gave each horse a hug and a pat. "How could I forget?" she said, laughing. "Oh, Mike, they look wonderful! Their coats are so shiny, like they've been polished."

"They have," Mike said. "Been polishin' 'em myself since early this morning. And they've been behavin' like a proper lady and gentleman, too." He untied The Ghost from a stout branch and handed the leadline to Val, holding on to Dancer himself. "Is it time yet?"

Val peered through the thick hedge, between the leaves and blossoms. "Yes — Miss Maggie's standing on a chair, trying to get everybody's attention."

When the talk and laughter had finally died down, Miss Maggie spoke. "I want to thank you all for coming here today, to honor Theodore and Catherine Taylor and their family," she said. "Young Theodore, Catherine, Erin, Teddy, Sparky, where are you?"

Doc and Catherine came forward hand in hand, and the children joined them next to Miss Maggie's chair as all the guests applauded and cheered.

"Where's Vallie?" Erin asked. "I don't see her anywhere."

"She'll be here in a minute," Miss Maggie told her. "Right now, I'd like to propose a toast — to the Taylors, all six of them!"

"Hear, hear!" roared Mayor Anderson, and everyone took a sip of champagne.

"Thank you, one and all," Doc said, putting his arm around Catherine's waist.

"And thank *you*, Miss Maggie, for the most wonderful wedding reception in the world," Catherine added, reaching up to squeeze the old lady's hand.

"Now everybody stay right where you are," Miss Maggie commanded as people began to move in the direction of the refreshment tables. Beaming down at Catherine and Doc, she said, "Valentine has a very special surprise for you both!" She turned to the rhododendron hedge. "Ready, Val?"

"Ready!" Val called back, and she and Mike led the horses around the hedge onto the sunlit lawn. All the guests murmured to each other, and Teddy shouted, "Vallie, what're your horses doing here?"

Their faces wreathed in smiles, Val and Mike brought The Ghost and Dancer right up to Doc and Catherine. "They're not *my* horses anymore," Val said as she handed The Ghost's lead to her father and Mike handed Dancer's to Catherine. "The Ghost is yours, Dad, and Dancer belongs to Catherine. They're my wedding gift to you!"

"Oh, Val!" Catherine gasped. "I — I don't know what to say!"

"Honey, are you sure you want to do this?" Doc said softly.

Miss Maggie hopped down from her chair and put her hands on her hips. "Of course she does, or she wouldn't have done it, right, Valentine?"

Val nodded happily. "I certainly can't ride two horses at the same time. But I'll keep taking care of them like always," she added. "And I imagine you'll let me ride them sometimes, won't you?" Looking from her father to her stepmother, she saw the stunned expressions on their faces, and her smile faded. "If you don't want them, that's okay, too," she said quickly.

"Not want them?" Catherine cried. "How could anybody not want a beautiful creature like this?" She stroked Dancer's arched neck, gazing at the mare in wonder. "A horse of my own! I never thought I'd see the day!"

"Honey, you couldn't have given us anything we wanted more," Doc said gruffly. He put an arm around Val, holding her close, and Catherine hugged her, too. The horses snorted and stamped, and the guests clapped and cheered even more loudly than they had before.

Val heaved a sigh of relief. "I'm so glad," she murmured. "Oh — there's something else!" She turned to Mike, who took a rumpled envelope out of his pocket and gave it to her. As Val presented the envelope to Catherine, she explained, "This is a letter from Paula Morgan, kind of like a gift certificate for five riding lessons each. I figure now that you have these terrific horses, you'd both better learn to be terrific riders!"

"Oh, Val, thank you! What wonderful presents!" Catherine said, kissing her on the cheek. Doc handed The Ghost's lead to Mike and gave her another hug, with both arms this time.

"Wonderful presents from a wonderful daughter," he said. "Thank you, honey. I love you very much. I love *all* of you very much," he added, releasing Val and opening his arms wide. Sparky, Teddy, and Erin rushed into his embrace. "There's no doubt about it, I'm the luckiest man in the world!"

"And I'm the luckiest woman," Catherine said, smiling at Val.

The crowd of guests surged across the lawn, eager to admire the horses and to offer yet more congratulations. Over the happy babble, Val heard someone calling her father's name, and she looked up to see Miss Maggie standing on the porch of her huge old house. She tugged at Doc's sleeve and he looked up, too. Miss Maggie was beckoning to him so he edged through the throng to find out what she wanted.

A moment later he was back. "Catherine," he said, making his way to his wife's side, "I don't know how to tell you this, but . . ." It was the first time in her life that Val had ever seen her father look sheepish.

"What is it, Ted? Nothing's wrong, is it?" Catherine asked anxiously.

Doc rubbed his beard. "Not unless you happen to be missing a cow," he said with a wry grin. "Miss Maggie just got a call from Trevor Merrill. He tracked me down, and he wants me to come to Longmeadow right away — it seems a cow fell into his swimming pool. He called the fire department to get her out, but she needs medical attention. So I'm very much afraid . . .''

Catherine sighed and rolled her eyes. ''That's what I get for marrying the only vet in Essex, Pennsylvania!'' she said, laughing. ''Is your medical bag in the car?''

''Yes, it is,'' Val said. ''I put it there, just in case. Dad, can I go with you? Maybe I can help!''

''Me, too!'' Toby had heard the whole conversation, and now he came over next to Val. ''Who knows? It might be one of *our* cows!''

''Sure, Toby. Come on, Vallie. Let's go!'' Doc gave Catherine a quick kiss. ''You understand, don't you dear? This shouldn't take very long. We should be back in no time flat.''

Smiling, Catherine said, ''Of course I understand, Ted. Now hurry up and take care of that poor beast.''

''Don't worry about your horses,'' Mike said. ''We'll keep an eye on them till you get back, won't we, kids?''

''We sure will,'' Sparky said, and Teddy and Erin nodded.

Doc strode across the lawn, heading for his car. Val and Toby followed, but Val found herself falling behind because the heels of her pink linen pumps kept sinking into the grass.

''Hey, wait for me!'' she shouted. She bent down, took off her shoes, and carried them in her hand as she hurried to catch up. "You don't think the cow is drowned, do you, Dad?" she asked as the three of them got into the car.

"I doubt it, or Mr. Merrill wouldn't have bothered to call," Doc said. "But she may be in pretty bad shape. We won't know until we get there. Everybody in? Seat belts fastened? Then let's get going!"

Everything's different and yet everything's still the same, Val thought as they sped down Miss Maggie's driveway to the road that would take them to Longmeadow Farms. It was business as usual for Dr. Theodore Taylor and his two young assistants at Animal Inn!